I0658441

The Agreement

After the Handshake, Life Was Never the Same

By Rovel D. Simmons

Tragedy to Triumph Books, Inc

Fairview Heights, Il

The Agreement
After the Handshake, Life Was Never the Same
Volume 2

Cover Illustration by Chris House of Inkosi Design Studio
Book Design by Outskirts Press, Inc.

Tragedy to Triumph Books, Inc
Fairview Heights, Il

ISBN- 13: 978-0-9791589-0-2

Contact the author directly at:
rooseveltsimmons86@gmail.com

Acknowledgments

First, I would like to thank God for giving me strength and courage and for surrounding me with inspiring, high-quality people. You know who you are and thank you very much for putting up with me.

Of course, I must thank you for purchasing this book. I believe you will enjoy the story. Hopefully, I will see you at the end, when you visit my Web site and record your positive comments in my Guest Book.

Thank you ahead of time.

Visit the Web site: www.theagreement123.com

Oh, yeah! I almost forgot. I would like to thank everybody who visited me and sent me "Get well!" wishes following my near-death experience. If you would like to know more about my near-death experience, visit the site and click on the icon "Near Death Experience."

Chapter 1

Attention!

"Attention all units! Neighbors say shots were fired at 2116 Barry Avenue. Neighbors reported hearing loud noises and arguments at the house for at least an hour. One person appears to have been injured. We have no word of his condition yet, " reported a dispatcher after receiving a very disturbing phone call. Several units responded to the call with emergency lights and sirens.

"Units there is an ambulance in route," the dispatcher continued.

This is what took place after a shooting at our house in the suburbs. When the police arrived, four people were in the house — two men, a young boy, and a lady. One of the men went to the hospital. Four Everyone else went to the police station.

When we got to the station, we were asked to sit down in a small room without a picture on the wall. hard, steel chairs are piled in the corner. Three detectives were in the room. One stood with a cup of coffee in his hand, staring at us. The other two looked like rookies, ready to take orders.

"Okay, who wants to start talking first? You all have heard your rights. Right?" asked the detective who stood with the cup in his hand.

We all looked at the detective and nodded our heads in agreement.

"Okay. Start from the beginning. Take your time. We've got all day."

"I will do all the talking," proclaimed the man of the house.

"The rest of you may jump in whenever you feel it's necessary," the chief detective responded as he looked at the lady and child for confirmations. "Go ahead, sir. Again, how did this start?"

"Well, it all started with Mr. Smith."

Chapter 2

Mr. Smith

Mr. Smith had just received a well paying job as a janitor, and he appeared to like it a lot. He did a very good job, so much so that at the end of the work day, he was filthy. This is the highest paying job Mr. Smith had ever. He finally will have enough money to have a fun day with his son. After work, he plans to take him to McDonald's and a movie. He'd never had enough money to do this before. While he mopped the floor, his son was at home, worrying his mother by continually asking her the time.

Mr. Smith took a break for lunch. While he chewed his sandwich, he noticed a co-worker eating lunch and reading the pages of a newspaper that were scattered on a table.

"You mind sharing your paper?" Mr. Smith asked, staring at the entertainment section.

"No, I don't mind," replied his co-worker.

Mr. Smith grabbed the entertainment section to

see the times of the show. *Oh, good! The show doesn't start until 8:30. That will allow me lots of time to get home and take my shower and take my son to McDonald's,* he thought.

The horn blew, signaling that lunch was over, and Mr. Smith wasted no time getting back to diligently mopping the floor.

Meanwhile, a co-worker approached him. "Mr. Smith the boss, (Mr. Washington) told me to tell you that he would like to see you at the end of the day."

"I hope it's to give me a raise," he said, mopping steadily. "Although, I have only been working here for two weeks."

"Well, I don't know what it's for. He just told me to tell you."

Mr. Smith nods and the co-worker walked around the mop bucket to the restroom. Mr. Smith stayed focused and kept mopping until the horn blew to announce the end of the day. He thought about changing clothes before going to see the boss, as his co-worker had told him to do. Then he realized that it might take him too long, and he didn't think it would be wise to keep the boss waiting. Plus Mr. Washington would know how hard he worked when he saw his filthy clothes. When he arrived at Mr. Washington's office, the door was open a crack.

"Hey! I see you got the message that I needed to see you, " said the boss when he saw Mr. Smith peep through the crack.

"Uh, yes sir, " Mr. Smith uttered nervously because he did not have a good feeling about this meeting. It was like a déjà vu.

"Have a seat," the boss said, extending his hand and pointing at the chair.

"No, no! I will stay standing, because I don't want to get your furniture dirty."

"Yeah, judging by how dirty you are, you appear to be a really hard worker," he replied with a raised eyebrow. "That's why it's really hurts me to tell you this."

Mr. Smith sighed.

"Well here it goes. Due to a cancelled contract, our compensation expense is way over budget. Therefore, I have to lay you off for now."

"Lay me off! " Mr. Smith replied. "Please don't do that. I've only had this job for two weeks." He raised two fingers to show his time on the job.

"That's why we have to lay you off, because you are at the bottom of the seniority list. I am so sorry. But we sure will call you back if we get another contract."

"All right. But are you sure?" Mr. Smith said, looking disappointed.

The boss nodded his head to say yes and frowned. "I am so sorry," he added.

Mr. Smith left the office very upset and disappointed. He was in shock and felt that he had nowhere to turn. Then he noticed an advertisement for liquor. *There is a liquor store right below the ad,* he thought. He walked to the store and asked the cashier for two pints of their hardest liquor. After paying for his purchase, he left the store and walked over to a bus stop bench. He sat, drinking and wondering what had just happened. He forgot all about the promise he had made to his son.

A bus stopped and the driver opened the door for him to get on. He waved the bus off. He did this repeatedly, and as time went by, the more he drank, the less willing he became to go home and face his girlfriend to tell her the bad news. Another bus stopped and opened the door for him to get on. He decided to take this one, having no idea where it was going. He just wanted to get as far away as he could. That is exactly what happened, because without realizing it, he had boarded the express bus to the suburbs. During the drive, he constantly sneaked drinks. By the time the bus reached the suburbs, he suddenly remembered the promise he made to his son.

"Damn!" he cursed. "Bus driver, let me off at your very next stop!"

He got up and tripped over himself. He didn't realize that he was drunk. He held the rails until it was time to get off. Once on the sidewalk, he started talking to himself.

"Man! Where am I?"

He then noticed a bus stop across the street. Without looking from left to right, he attempted to cross the street. I say attempted, because an oncoming car just missed him, and he fell to the ground.

"Wow! That was close," said Mr. Smith as he looked at himself to make sure he wasn't hurt.

He stared at the car and saw someone turning around to make sure he was all right. The car never stopped, and Mr. Smith wondered if it would ever stop. It never did.

"Man! What kind of people are they? I hope they never need anything from me, " he said to himself. Then he realized that he was sitting on the street. When he attempted to stand up, he stumbled, but this time he wasn't so lucky. A car full of teenagers struck him and left him unconscious. Someone called 911. When the ambulance arrived, they found no identification on him. You see, Mr. Smith had left his wallet in his locker at work along with his clean change of clothes.

Chapter 3

The Johnsons

I can't tell you who hit Mr. Smith, but I do know the people who almost hit him. I know what was going on at the time and why they couldn't stop. Earlier that evening, the driver of the car was a wealthy man name Mr. Johnson. Mr. Johnson and his wife were rushing their son to the hospital. This is what happened that day. Mr. Johnson had come home from work, called his son, and wondered why his son didn't answer him. He became very frustrated and went after him.

"Boy, don't you hear me calling your name?" Mr. Johnson asked as he turned down the volume on the TV with the remote. "Boy, I said get up! Let's go eat. Get up! " He nudged him. "Why aren't you answering me? What's wrong with your eyes? Are you sick?" Then he yelled, "Honey, get in here!"

Mrs. Johnson dropped her fork and knife and ran into the room to see what was so important.

"What's wrong?" she asked. She glanced at her son. He looked like he was asleep.

"It's Tim! He won't get up."

"What do you mean, he won't get up? He's probably just tired from a long day in school."

"No! I have been screaming and hollering, and he hasn't said a word or even moved."

Mrs. Johnson reached down to check Tim's neck for a pulse. She found a pulse, but something told her things weren't right.

"I'm going to get the car ready." Mr. Johnson said as he pulled the keys out of his pocket.

Mrs. Johnson put on her clothes and her son's clothes. She closed her eyes and said a short prayer for her son. "Heavenly Father, please don't let anything happen to my son. He is all I got."

"Okay. Are you ready? Is everything ready to go? " Mr. Johnson cut in.

He picked up his only son to carry him to the car.

"I will lock up and be right out," Mrs. Johnson said while getting the rest of her son's things.

Mrs. Johnson locked the door, ran to the car, and jumped in the back seat. She thought it would be wise for someone to sit with her baby. Mr. Johnson backed up without looking for passing traffic. He put the car in drive and peeled rubber. He ran stop signs and became eager to run traffic lights. The only reason he didn't was that there was oncoming traffic. When the light changed to green, he was swift to pass other cars. As a matter of fact, he drove so fast that he came very close to hitting someone.

"You see that?" Mr. Johnson asked.

"Yeah, he was a bum, right?"

Mr. Johnson moved his shoulders up and down to say "I don't know."

"Well, please don't stop. We've got to get our son treated," Mrs. Johnson replied, as she looked back and noticed the bum sitting up on the street. She sighed with relief. "He's sitting up. You didn't hit him."

They maneuvered their way through traffic and finally made it to the hospital. Mr. Johnson and his wife sat in the emergency waiting room. Their son was in a room with Mr. Johnson's doctor. About two hours later, another emergency came in from an ambulance. Mr. Johnson got a glimpse at the guy.

"Honey, did you see that guy?" He asked while following the stretcher with his eyes.

"It looked like that bum you almost hit!"

"Yeah, it did. I thought you said that you saw him standing up.

Mrs. Johnson put her hand on his thigh to assure him. "I did. Besides, there was no bang, so if we did hit him it wasn't that hard. That guy who came in looked like he was about to die."

"Okay. Well, someone else must have hit him."

"I hope he is okay," Mrs. Johnson said sincerely.

"Well, hopefully they won't take their attention from our son. I would like to know that our son's life will be more important than the life of some old bum," Mr. Johnson replied.

They sat in complete silence. Mr. Johnson daydreamed and subconsciously listened to the receptionist as she talked on the phone. She appeared to be angry about something.

"Girl! You mean to tell me your man couldn't come back to watch his son so you could go to work? And he promised to take him to McDonald's and a movie, too? Are you going to take him yourself? Girl, I told you to leave him a long time ago. I mean, who needs an irresponsible man? Hey, I will fill in for you. We already had two emergencies. I don't expect anymore tonight. So go take care of your son, and don't worry. We will find some good men one day."

The doctor walked into the waiting room and took Mr. Johnson's attention away from the receptionist.

"Well, your son is suffering from his heart condition," said Dr. Cashion, holding a clipboard with paperwork. "Due to the late stage of the illness, your son needs an immediate transplant or he may not make it."

"What do you mean?" Mr. Johnson said with a raised brow.

Mrs. Johnson started to cry.

"My secretary put the word out already. She

will immediately contact me when she knows something," said the doctor.

A nurse came rushing in. "Doctor, you are needed right away in the emergency room!"

"Can we see him?" asked Mr. Johnson.

"I don't see why not. I will have the nurse to take you to see him. However, I must warn you that he is hooked up to a lot of machines. He is also still asleep."

Dr. Cashion rushed away, putting on his gloves and placing a mask over his face. The nurse escorted the two to their son's room. Mrs. Johnson cried all the way to the door, and cried out louder when she saw him. Mr. Johnson put his arms around her to console her.

"Come on! Get it together before you go in. You don't want to upset him even more," Mr. Johnson said as he helped her wipe her tears.

Moments later, the doctor came in to speak to Mr. and Mrs. Johnson. He asked if he could speak to them privately. A nurse appeared to be checking Tim's vital signs. She hooked up the last tube and excused herself.

"Can you close the door behind you?" the doctor asked the nurse as he walked in from the emergency. "Mr. and Mrs. Johnson, I may have found a heart for your son. We may have a donor if the man I am talking about doesn't wake up any time soon."

"You mean you don't know if he's a donor

yet? " asked Mr. Johnson with his hands on his side. "Where did you get this match?"

"He just came in."

"Who, the bum? " asked Mr. Johnson.

"I guess. Do you know him?"

"No, not really. But we almost ran over him on the way here."

"How do you know he's a bum? Have you ever seen him around here?"

"No, no, doctor. He just looked like one because of the dirty clothes and the bottle in his hand."

"Anyway, there is still a fifty-fifty chance that this guy can make it. But if he doesn't, we can use his heart for your son. He is currently on a life-support machine. He is fighting for his life. He must have something to live for, " said the doctor with deep stares.

"Beep, beep, beep," his heart monitor is going off. The doctor rushed to their son and nurses came to assist him.

"We must ask you all to step outside," the nurse said as she escorted them to the door and closed it behind them.

Chapter 4

The Exchange Agreement

Mr. Smith continued to lie in his unconscious state. Meanwhile, the doctor and some of the nurses come out of the room after treating the Johnsons' son. Dr. Cashion stopped to speak with them.

"Your son's body didn't like the medicine we were giving him. He had a strong reaction to it. I am afraid if we don't find a match for him very soon, he may die in a couple of days."

"What about the guy who came in earlier?" Mr. Johnson asked with a raised brow.

"What about him? " replied the doctor, as he shrugged his shoulder. "I can't do anything with him now. We are still waiting for consent from a family member. We still don't know who this guy is or where he came from. So we must wait until a family member contacts us or we contact them." "But suppose he wakes up?" responded Mr. Johnson.

"Then there is nothing we can do."

Mr. and Mrs. Johnson gave the doctor a pathetic look.

"I need to do something," said Mr. Johnson. "Doctor, can I see you in your office?"

Dr. Cashion looked at him sincerely and turned towards the hallway door. They walked to the doctor's office, and Mrs. Johnson stayed with her son.

"You mind closing the door?" Mr. Johnson asked as he entered the office ahead of the doctor.

"No, I don't mind," the doctor replied.

"All right, doctor. Name your price. There is nothing too large for my son's life."

"Man! I can't take money from you."

"Man, we are talking about my son."

Mr. Johnson took out a sheet of paper and wrote the amount of $200,000. Dr. Cashion saw it and was pleased. He started to think about his drug habit. Then he asked for more. He took the paper and wrote a larger amount. Even though the first number was suitable, he thought he would request more for his ego. He countered with $250,000. Mr. Johnson looked at the number and agreed without hesitation.

"All right!"

"If I do this, we can get into a lot of trouble.

This is basically murder. Hell, I can lose my license." said the doctor when it finally hit him what he was about to do.

"I know, and I certainly appreciate this," said Mr. Johnson, looking at the doctor sincerely. "Well, I have to get back to my wife and son. Do we have an agreement?" Mr. Johnson extended his hand for the doctor to shake it. As they shook hands, Mr. Johnson continued, "Don't worry. I will do everything I can to help you cover this up. And since we just shook on it, I just gave you my word." He looked at the doctor, realizing that the doctor was really unsure about doing such a thing. "Look, you may not want to take a chance, but I don't want to take a chance and lose my son. I think the odds are working for me in this case."

There was silence, as the doctor went into deep thought.

"Come on, doctor. This is my son. He is all I got! This man probably doesn't have one person who cares about him."

Mr. Smith continued looking at the doctor's uncertain face.

"All right. I will do it. When can you deliver the funds?"

"When can you deliver the heart?"

"We will wait at least twenty-four hours for someone to miss him or to find out who this person is. So we are looking at tomorrow at 6:00 in the evening. And please don't share this with anyone.

Not even your wife!"

"Alright. Thank you! Thank you! Thank you! You are a life-saver. Literally, doctor, you are, " Mr. Johnson said with a sigh of relief.

"Now remember Mr. Johnson, even if things go well, I still can't promise you that he is going to live long. But I do know that he will live longer then what he's got now."

"But sometimes people live longer than expected—even to old age, right?" Mr. Johnson replied, looking anxiously for the doctor to agree.

Dr. Cashion nodded his head in agreement.

"Well, something is better than nothing. We can't sit here and let him die," Mr. Johnson continued.

"I understand," the doctor replied as he stood up to escort the man out the door. "Can you and your wife come back tomorrow to complete some paper work —that is if no one claims John Doe?"

"We will be here all day, so I will see you tomorrow."

"We will have to do the surgery tomorrow, so be prepared for a very long day."

Chapter 5

Pat and John Doe

The next day, the Johnsons arrived back at the hospital and sat down to complete the paper work. They heard activity in the background. A girl named Pat had just arrived at work to relieve her co-worker, Janice.

"Hey, sorry about yesterday," said Pat.

"Have you heard from him? " asked Janice, expecting a negative reply.

"No. I believe he got paid yesterday and decided to party his money away. His butt probably relapsed!"

"Girl! Just worry about you and your child for now. How did your son take it?"

"He is stunned, and he appeared to be very disappointed," Pat rebutted with a sad expression.

"Who's got him now? " Janice asked as she put her things away.

"He is with his father's mother. I took him over

there in case his father decides to come over there after a long night. That way, he can see the disappointment on his son's face."

"Good! Well, here. Can you take these papers to the front circulation desk in ICU on the fourth floor? This will give me time to clean up and prepare the area for you."

"Sure," Pat replied.

She walked to the elevator and took it to the fourth floor. On her way back, she heard a heart monitor go off in one of the rooms. All hospital staff had been trained to offer immediate assistance if this happened when they were around. When she attempted to go in, a nurse stopped her at the door.

"Hey! Excuse me. We got it, " the nurse said, pushing her back with her hand. She closed the door and walked out with Pat.

"How come it's going to the second stage? That person is dying," Pat replied as she was being scooted out the door.

"Hey are you a nurse?"

Pat motioned her head to say no. "Well, I said we got it. Now, here! Take this heart and give it to the donor lab on the second floor so they can get it ready for the recipient."

"Okay. Sorry, I didn't mean to give you a hard time," said Pat looking very sincere.

As she took the heart to the lab, she noticed a tag that read John Doe. Something moved inside her, but she decided to ignore the feeling. *This could be anybody,* she thought. She went to the waiting room for a snack before starting her workday. There, she overheard Mr. Johnson and his wife talking together in the lobby area.

"Honey, I did what I had to do for our son, " Mr. Johnson said as he looked into space.

"Please! I am not interested in knowing what you did. I forgive you, and I am sure our son will forgive you, as well."

"I did what I had to do for our son, " Mr. Johnson repeated as he continued to stare.

"All right, baby. I know you did. " She placed her hand on his thigh again to reassure him.

Pat left the room, wishing that her boyfriend had the same kind of heart that Mr. Johnson had. Then she thought, *Forget John! I know I am going to find me another man. He is just no good!* She returned to the front desk.

"What took you so long?" the night receptionist asked?

"I had to drop this heart off to the lab."

"You mean to tell me they found a heart for that kid already? That's great! I just saw the couple in the hallway. I was wondering what was going on."

"You mean that man and his wife in the lobby? That man was so fine," she said, giving her co-worker a high-five. "He was such a gentleman, too. I heard them discussing their child and how he had to do what he had to do for his son. I wish John was like him."

"Keep dreaming," the receptionist said, poking her lips out and rolling her eyes. "Did you hear if their son was going to be all right?"

"Yeah, it sound liked he was. But the man kept saying that he had to do what he had to do. I wonder what he meant," she looked puzzled.

Chapter 6

He Is Going to Be All Right! Right?

Dr. Cashion walked into the waiting room after treating Tim Johnson. He noticed Mr. and Mrs. Johnson sitting in the corner by the snack machine. Mr. Johnson stood when he saw him. "What's up? " he shouted.

"I believe he's going to be all right, provided that there are no complications. He will have to take his medication until further notice," the doctor said, staring shamefully at Mr. Johnson. He knew what he had done was wrong.

"Thank you, Jesus!" said Mrs. Johnson. "Can we see him?"

"Sure. This way, " the doctor said, extending his hand to show them the direction.

They went to the lab and helped each other put on protective clothes. Then they walked towards their son's room. When they arrived, Mrs. Johnson looked at her son. He was sound asleep, as if he was a newborn baby again in his baby cubicle. She started to think of that day.

Chapter 7

When He Was Born

It was very early in the morning, and Mrs. Johnson's water had just broken. "Honey, I think my water broke."

"Hmmm. " Mr. Johnson turned to reposition himself to rub her stomach, but he was falling back to sleep.

"Man, get off me! I don't need a rub. I need a doctor!"

"A doctor? What you need to go see a doctor for? " he mumbled in his sleep.

"I told you, my water just broke!" Mrs. Johnson hit him to wake him up.

"You what? Oh, Damn! Let me get my clothes on and I will help you get yours on in a minute."

"Baby, I think I am going just like this," she looked down to see if her sweat pants and T-shirt looked all right.

"Okay. Stay there and I will get the car ready," he replied while nervously tripping over the trashcan.

"Dude! What are you doing?" Mrs. Johnson asked when she heard the noise.

Mr. Johnson smiled, because he had never heard her use slang.

"Dude!" he said under his breath with a smile as he hurried downstairs to get their coats and keys. Then he ran back upstairs.

"Honey, are you ready?" Mr. Johnson asked, breathing very hard.

Mrs. Johnson grabbed her stomach. "Yeah. I just hope the baby is patient enough to wait until we get to the hospital."

"Me, too, " Mr. Johnson replied.

He helped her downstairs and into the car. When Mr. Johnson tried to fasten her seatbelt, she hit his hand. "Will you just drive? Man, I am not that helpless."

They arrived at the hospital, and the receptionist saw that she was about to have a baby. She called a nurse to get a wheelchair for Mrs. Johnson. Then she asked about their insurance and other matters. When they were done, she gathered the paperwork and said, "Well, that's it! So, is this your first one?"

"If it's a boy, then it's probably my last one, depending on how this labor turns out."

"Let me know how the pain is, because I will be having my first child in seven months."

"Sure, if I see you."

"Now, where do we go? " Mr. Johnson asked to

stop all the girl-talk and get things rolling.

"The nurse will be here shortly to take you to your room. Good luck!"

"Don't say that! Luck doesn't have anything to do with life!" Mrs. Johnson rebutted.

Mrs. Johnson didn't go into labor until that afternoon. The baby was born around three o'clock —3:14 p.m., to be exact. At that time, he went through some serious heart problems. The obstetrician spent hours trying to get his breathing under control.

"Hey! Hey! Hey! " Mr. Johnson yelled, trying to get Mrs. Johnson's attention.

"What?" She responded taking her mind away from her deep thought but never taking her eyes off her sick son. At this point, she couldn't dream of leaving her son's bedside. Her husband felt the same.

"Honey, I am going to check into a room for us at the hotel across the street."

While walking through the waiting room, the announcement of the news on the television set in the lobby reminded him how late it was in the evening. He checked his watch, and trotted to the hotel across the street.

Chapter 8

Coupons

"When the news came on, the top story was the unidentified man. This caught the attention of the on-duty receptionist. Pat listened as she did her work, not realizing that the broadcasters were talking about the man who had died in the hospital.

The news anchor announced, "This is our top story. An unidentified man, who was hit by an unidentified car yesterday, has passed. No one has come to identify the man up to now. Here is where you can help. Apparently, the man was supposed to go to McDonald's and the movies. We know this because they found in his pockets some coupon clippings for McDonald's and the movies. Anyone with information is asked to contact the Barry Police Department."

Pat overheard this message, stopped what she was doing, and started to pay more attention. The news anchor repeated her message, and in almost no time, a visitor arrived.

"Ma'am! Ma'am! Excuse me. Are you okay?" yelled the visitor.

When the news story was over and the channel went to a commercial, Pat noticed the visitor.

"Excuse me. I need to take a break," she responded as she got up and took her purse with her.

"What? Let me see your name tag. Pat, huh? I will see that you get fired for this," the visitor yelled with anger!

"Here. Complete these forms and someone will be here in a moment to help you further."

She asked a nurse to take her place while she went to the restroom. But she really went to call her son, Fred.

"Hello."

"Hello, son. Were you and your daddy supposed to go to the movies and McDonald's yesterday? And did you cut some coupons out of the paper?"

"Yes, Mama. I saw you do it before when you were going to buy groceries, and I thought I would cut some out for Dad to save him some money and to remind him about our movie date."

"Let me speak to your grandmom," she asked anxiously. "Son! Son! " she yelled before he put down the phone. "I love you."

"I Love you too, Mom. Hold on," Fred replied as he walked over to hand his grandmother the phone.

"Hello. Let me tell you what your son did. Hold on," she cut Grandma off. "Have you seen the news?"

"Yeah, I was watching it or hearing it when I was straightening up your son's mess."

"Well, first of all, have you seen or heard from your son?" Pat asked while she walked out of the bathroom to get more privacy when someone walked in.

"No! What did you see on the news, Pat? Is he okay?"

Grandma asked, holding her hand to her chest.

"Calm down, Mrs. Smith. Nothing is concrete yet. You may be wasting this stress. Please don't lose any sleep just yet. I will call you as soon as I hear something."

"Okay. Let me calm down before your son hears me, too," replied Grandma as she looked around the door to see where her grandson was. "Call me as soon as you hear something."

She hung up the phone, took a deep breath, and called the number the news asked the viewers to contact if they thought they might have information on the unidentified man.

"Hello. Barry Police Department," said the police secretary.

"Can I speak to whoever is in charge of the case of the unidentified man?"

"Please hold." The secretary pressed line 4 for the responding officer.

"Yes, May I help you?"

"Yes, I am calling about the unidentified man."

"Do you know him?" the officer asked eagerly. "I don't know," responded Pat, swallowing slowly. "Where is he?"

"The body is still at the hospital. Do you want me to meet you there? Where are you?"

"St. Mills Hospital."

"St. Mills!" the detective repeated sounding shocked.

"Yes! I work here."

"Well, this should be easy."

"Is he here?" Pat asked nervously.

"Yes, if you are calling from the St. Mills Hospital in the suburb of Barry. Here, do this. Go down to the morgue, take a look, and let me know."

"All right," Pat replied, and she swallowed again.

She hung up the phone, sighed, and looked at the elevators, wondering if she should take one or not.

At that moment, the visitor walked by. "Man there she goes again, staring in space. She should be a patient instead of a worker," he said sarcastically.

She paid no attention to his comment, stood up, and walked toward the elevator. The doors opened as soon as she pushed the down-arrow button. Inside, she hit the button for the bottom floor.

When the elevator reached her floor, a man in from the hall and pressed the stop button so she could exit.

"Are you coming out?" he asked, looking at her and narrowing his eyes.

"Uh, yeah. Thank you," she replied taking slow steps.

She looked down to the end of the hall and saw the door to the morgue. As she walked slowly in that direction, she heard someone talking on a phone.

"I am just saying if this person is unidentified, how do they know he was an organ donor? ... Whatever, but I have to go. Someone is here." He hung up the phone and looked up at Pat. "How can I help you?"

Pat looked at the morgue attendant. He was dressed in a white lab jacket.

"I am here to see the unidentified person," Pat said with her head down.

"Do you think you know him?"

"I don't know," she replied. "That's why I am here."

She rolled her eyes as he had asked was a stupid question.

"Okay. Well, let me see. John Doe is over here. Are you ready?" he asked as he grabbed the corner of the sheet, preparing to pull them back.

She nodded her head to say yes. The lab worker pulled back the sheet and Pat screamed very loud.

"NO! NO! NO! Why? Oh, why?"

"I guess you know him."

"Yes. He is my boyfriend."

"Oh, let me call the cops and let them know. What's his name?"

"John-n-n, " she cried. "His name is John Smith."

"Okay. I guess we had the John part right," he mumbled under his breath, smiling to himself.

Later, gossip circled around the hospital and the news got back to the doctor that someone knew the John Doe — rather, John Smith. The police arrived and asked Pat questions about Mr. Smith. One question that stuck in her mind was whether he was a donor. The doctor and three nurses asked her the same question.

Dr. Cashion went to his office and called Mr. Johnson.

Chapter 9

He Had a Girlfriend!

"Hello, Mr. Johnson? this is Dr. Cashion."
"Nothing is wrong with my son, is it?" asked Mr. Johnson in a frightened voice.

"No, he is fine. I am calling you to inform you that they found a family member. A young woman who works here at the hospital was his girlfriend."

"He had a girlfriend? ...With a job?"

"Yep. I am afraid we may have pulled the wrong cord on this one," said the doctor, wondering what would happen to him for his abominable act.

"Well, doc, was he a donor?"

"We don't know. We still haven't found his ID. But guess what else I found out?"

"What?"

"The man had a son?"

"Oh, no! What have we done?" Mr. Johnson replied sadly.

"Don't get worried yet. Everything will be all right as long as she doesn't start snooping."

Chapter 10

The Missing Wallet

"Hello. This is Mr. Washington, your son's boss. I am so sorry for your loss, Mrs. Smith."

"Thank you."

"Your son left his change of clothes here at work. Do you want someone to bring them to you?"

"Well, maybe I can ask his girlfriend to pick them up."

Moments later, Mr. Smith's girlfriend, Pat, arrived at the plant.

"Hi, I am here to pick up John's things," Pat said as she puts a bag on the counter.

"Okay, John Smith? All right. You know, I felt sorry for him. He was really a hard worker. Who are you to him?"

"I am his girlfriend and the mother of his child."

"Well, here is his stuff. Let us know when the

family makes arrangements, all right?"

As soon as she sat on the bus bench, Pat searched for John's wallet.

Let me see if I can answer that question they all asked at the hospital, she thought as she checked the pockets. She found the wallet, and his ID fell out. She picked it up and looked at it. "He was not a donor!" she yelled.

"What have they done?" She continued to yell. "Well I guess if he was already dead he wouldn't have minded. But what gave them the right? I am going to raise hell about this."

Chapter 11

Confronting the Doctor

Pat decided to catch the early bus to work in order to talk to the doctor. She walked in and knocked on the doctor's office door.

"Come in, " yelled Dr. Cashion.

Pat walked in and the doctor pointed his finger to the seat in front of his desk so she could sit down.

"You know, doc, he wasn't a donor," she said with her lips poked out.

"How do you know that?"

"It was on his driver's license," Pat responded.

"Do you have it? Where is it?"

"Here." She pulled John's ID out of her pocket and pointed at the spot reserved for donor objections. "You see this? It says no! Now, tell me what gave y'all the right to take his heart from him!"

"Tell me, how you knew his heart was taken."

"Because the nurse asked me to take the heart

down to the lab, and the name on the bag read John Doe. My boyfriend was the only person here by that name."

"I see you've done your research," the doctor responded looking impressed.

"What gave you the right?" Pat asked, looking at the doctor with disappointment in her eyes.

"He was already dead."

"Yeah, right! I heard him flat line after you guys had taken his heart out, so he couldn't have been dead. I am going to sue this hospital's pants off, and you are going to jail for murder," she shouted! She jumped up and stormed out of the office.

When she was out of sight, the doctor phoned the human resources office and asked for her records. A worker brought him the folder, and as he read the file in search of her address, he ran across an entry detailing her past involvement in a 12-step program for drug rehabilitation. This gave him an idea. He called a man named Ted.

Meanwhile, Pat returned to the emergency room desk. She sat down at her station and started to reflect on her good memories with Mr. Smith, such as the first time they met and when she found out she was pregnant with their son.

Chapter 12

The Day They Met

Mr. Smith was walking downtown one fine summer evening. Mr. Smith noticed someone staring at him and coming towards him. "Hey, man! What's up with you? " asked the staring man.

Mr. Smith looked hard to make sure he recognized him. Then he said, "Hey, Ted! What's up with you, man? " He greeted the man with a cool handshake and a handshake hug.

"Nothing much, man. Where are you coming from, all suited up? " Ted replied as he checked Mr. Smith out and closed the middle button of his sports jacket.

"Job hunting," Smith replied, lifting his briefcase.

"Job hunting! Man, you can work for me! " said Ted, pressing his right hand to his chest.

"No thanks! I know what you do."

"I know you do. You used to be my favorite customer."

"Are you still in the pharmaceutical business?" John asked with a smile.

"Man! Whatever man! You need a job or what?" he pulled out a roll of money.

"I'll take the what!" Mr. Smith replied as he stared at the money and smiled again.

"Man, whatever! Anyway, if you ever need me, you know how to reach me. You know I still owe you for taking up for me when I was in high school. I owe you my life; so if there is anything I can do for you, I will do what I have to do. I am a true man of my word."

Mr. Smith gave him a "whatever" look.

While they continued to talk, a woman came up from the street.

"Hi Ted," she said as she walked by.

She looked as if she worked in the health profession. Mr. Smith couldn't take his eyes off her. He nudged Ted, trying to get Ted to introduce them. Ted got the cue.

"Hey, this is my friend, John," he said. "Can you talk to him for a minute? I'll be right back."

Ted disappeared in the crowd.

"So hi! Are you a businessman?" she asked looking at him up and down and checking out his suit.

"Mr. Smith thought that since he didn't know the nice-looking young lady, he would tell her a lie."

"Yes, yes. I am a businessman," Mr. Smith said, looking confident.

"Are you in pharmaceutical sales like Ted?" "Ha! Ha! No. Let's just say I got my own cleaning service." He chuckled again.

"What's so funny?" she asked, narrowing her eyes.

"Nothing, I asked Ted if he was still in pharmaceutical sales, too."

"Oh! I guess we have the same jokes. Speaking of Ted, can you tell him I will holla at him later, because my bus is coming?"

"Oh, I am catching the same bus, " he said gladly.

"How do you have your own business and not have a car?" she asked, clinching her mouth in disbelief.

"I just started it."

"Come on! We can finish talking on the bus." The lady looked at him as if she knew he was pulling her leg.

The bus pulled up right in front of Mr. Smith. He stepped back and allowed her to board first. They walked to the back, found an empty seat, and sat together.

"So, where do you work?" Mr. Smith asked.

"I am an emergency room receptionist at a hospital in the suburbs."

"I bet you see some wild things working there," he said.

She replied, smacking her lips, "I said the suburbs. Most of what we get is heart attacks and little children coming in with colds. But it's become a little wild since I started working evenings. I just had emergency ICU training, too."

"What's that for? " he asked.

"That's for when a heart monitor goes off in a patient's room. Now, I am allowed to go in and help. I can't wait until I am given the chance to help save someone's life."

"Oh, okay," he replied, intrigued by this young lady's character.

They continued their conversation, and Mr. Smith realized that she was a good catch, especially when he found out that she had a good job. But he couldn't help wondering how she knew Ted or what their relationship was. When he asked, she didn't comment much and only said they where old friends. Anyway, Mr. Smith and the stranger were so engrossed in conversation that they didn't realize that they had not exchange names.

"Did I ask you your name?" Mr. Smith asked.

"No you didn't. It's Pat, by the way."

"Oh, Okay. I'm John. John Smith."

"Okay, Mr. Smith," Pat replied with a smile. "Ted said when he introduced us that your name was John. But he didn't tell me about Smith."

Mr. Smith returned the smile.

They exchanged phone numbers and dated ever since then. By the time she realized that he didn't have his own business, she was already in love and pregnant.

Since nothing was going on in the emergency room that day, Pat's mind started to wander off again. She started thinking about when she became pregnant with her son, Fred.

Chapter 13

The Conception of Mr. Smith's Son, Fred

"Oh no, no! It can't be." Pat exclaimed. She was in the restroom taking a pregnancy test. After a pause, she decided to try a different brand to make sure. She got the same results. "Damn!" She picked up the phone to call her friend.

"Girl, you won't believe this," Pat sounded disappointed.

"What? You pregnant? Just kidding. I know you are very careful when it comes to that." "I wish it were a joke."

"What?"

"Yeah, I must have slipped."

"Are you sure? Your period might be late."

"It's been two weeks!" Pat replied. "I've never been that late."

"Well, what test did you take? I hope you didn't

take one of those cheap ones."

"I took two name brands and they both said the same thing."

"Wow! I guess ... Congratulations! Have you told him yet?"

"Who? My boyfriend? Girl, I know that he's not ready for a child. He can barely take care of himself, having a job here and a job there."

"Well, you are going to have to tell him eventually."

"Not if ..."

"Oh, you will go there for real!"

"Hell, yeah! I will. You know I don't want any kids out of wedlock, and John is in no position to get married."

"Well, girl, I don't know, but if I was him, I would like to know, because his job situation could change tomorrow."

"We are going to let tomorrow take care of itself. Now, do you think you can go with me to the clinic?"

"Yeah, I guess."

Three weeks later, Pat's friend picked her up to take her to the clinic.

"Hey, girl! Are you ready?" her friend asked.

"Yeah. I may need to make a stop before I go. I need to get a high."

"But you are pregnant!" her friend replied angrily.

"Girl, I am not going to be pregnant that long,

so don't even trip."

During the ride, Pat hollered when she saw the drug dealer. She didn't care that he appeared to be making a transaction with someone who looked as if he didn't want to be recognized.

"Hey, you got something for me? " she called.

"Pat, is that you?"

"John, what are you doing here?"

"I was about to ask you the same thing."

Pat's friend nudged her. "You know you were meant to run into him. If you don't tell him, I will!"

"Girl, all right. I will tell him. Honey, come here. I got something to tell you."

"Hey, y'all can take care of that lovey-dovey stuff later. Now, what do you need?" asked the drug dealer, anxious to make a deal.

"Man, I will share mines with her, all right," John replied. They gave each other dap.

"I'll holla, " the drug dealer replied. He started to walk towards some people who he thought he knew on the corner. But before he reached them, he turned around with a disappointed face. "You know, it's kind of upsetting to see that you all are back smoking. You all are good people. I thought you'd be strong for each other. But John, I am always going to have your back because of our agreement."

The drug dealer walked away, and someone else approached him for a transaction.

"So Pat, honey, what's up? " Her friend looked

at Pat with a serious expression. Pat got out of the car to stand face-to-face with John.

"Well, honey, let me just say it. I haven't had a period in two months."

John smiled. Then, when he looked harder at Pat, he frowned.

"So, you are not happy about this?"

"You mean to tell me you are? " Pat replied with wide eyes.

"Hell, yeah!"

"How are you going to take care of a baby when you only have a job every now and then? As a matter of fact, how come you aren't at work right now?"

John looked down.

"Don't tell me! See, that's why I am going to get an abortion."

John looked up with a pitiful face. "Girl, please don't do that to my baby. Please, I will do better."

"Are you going to do better by doing drugs again?"

"No. I thought I would get high before I gave you the bad news."

"Well, the same is true for me. I thought I would get high before I get rid of this child."

"Look, I don't think it was a coincidence that I ran into you like this. And since we did, can you just give me a chance. Something will come through. Please don't do this." He grabbed her and hugged her. She hugged him back.

"All right. I guess I can ... " a slight moment of silence ... "Dad. " Pat tilts her head back, gets eye contact with John and smiles.

"Thank you! Thank you! I promise I will be there for both of you.... I guess we don't need these anymore."

Pat looked down in his hand and saw the ice. "I guess not, " she responded.

He threw the drugs on the ground.

Pat heard the sound of the phone ringing on her desk. It brought her back to today. She answered. It was Mr. Smith's mother.

"Honey, I am just calling to make sure you are all right."

"Grandma, something is wrong and I can't put my finger on it."

"Well, knowing you, I am sure you will get to the bottom of it."

"Well ... " The phone rang again. A caller was on the other line.

"Hold on, Grandma."

"Yes, " Pat told the caller. "Hold on, doctor."

"Grandma, I have to go downstairs to get a file for the doctor."

"Is that your job?"

"No, not really, but we do it sometimes because no file clerk is on duty this late and we are slow."

"All right, girl. Be careful, because I remember you telling me how isolated and scary it is downstairs."

"Yeah, you're right, but I should be all right. Bye. " Pat sighed and got up to go downstairs.

Meanwhile, the doctor was upstairs calling Mr. Johnson to tell him what he had just heard from Mr. Smith's girlfriend that Mr. Smith was not a donor.

Chapter 14

A Little Over-excited

Mr. Johnson and his son were watching a football game and talking noisily. "Dad, I am still trying to figure out why are you a Dallas fan, " his son said sarcastically.

"You will find out when they beat your team again."

"You know any team that plays Dallas is my team," his son said before taking a sip of the Kool-Aid his mother had made for him earlier.

"Son, why do you want to play against your Dad?"

"I am not playing against you, Dad. I am playing against Dallas."

Mrs. Johnson walked in holding a pitcher of Kool-Aid.

"Son, do you want some more Kool-Aid?"

"Yes, Mom."

Mrs. Johnson looked at Mr. Johnson. "Sorry! I don't make Kool-Aid for Dallas fans." They all started to laugh. Then Dallas made a touchdown, and Mr. Johnson hollered with excitement.

"Yeah! This is why I am a Dallas fan, " Mr. Johnson said proudly.

Mrs. Johnson and her son looked at each other and smirked.

"Son, why are you still in your Sunday clothes?" she asked, changing her tone.

"Oh, I am sorry. I will take them off. In the meantime, can you make sure Dallas doesn't cheat?"

She smiled and nodded yes. Tim walked to his room to change his clothes.

"Honey you missed your son in the children's choir today," she said while turning down the TV with the remote.

"Did he have a solo?"

"No!"

"Well, I am sure that he was just moving his lips. Anyway, what was the service about today?"

"It was about the Ten Commandments. Oh yeah, my spirit moved when we were talking about thou shall not kill." She looked at Mr. Johnson and he just stared at the TV.

"Honey, I am watching the game and I don't want to talk about that now. Besides, we weren't the ones who killed him anyway," he said without taking his eyes off the TV.

"Yeah, but we were involved."

"Catch the ball, fool! Oh, I am sorry did you say something."

The phone rang and Mrs. Johnson answered it.
"Honey, it's for you, " she said, extending her arm to hand him the phone.

"Don't they know the game is on? This had better be important. Hello!"

"Hey! Sorry for calling you on a Sunday, but I just wanted to tell you that Mr. John Doe wasn't a donor."

"Doctor, how did you find that out?"

"His girlfriend just told me, and she is pissed!"

"Oh! How did she find out about the transplant?"

"Well like I said, she works here, and somehow, she was up on the floor during the time of the operation."

"Uh ... are you going to be all right? I am so sorry."

There is a moment of silence, and then the doctor replied.

"Don't worry. I checked her records and she was referred here from Try Again Rehab."

"Oh! She was on that stuff."

"Was!"

"Okay, doctor. I don't want to know what's up your sleeves. So, I will—"

At that moment, Mr. Johnson's son exclaimed in pain, interrupting their conversation.

"Ah! " he yelled, grabbing his chest.

"Is everything okay?" Mrs. Johnson called out, nervously.

"Hold on, doctor! Son, are you okay?"

"Yeah, I think I just got a little too excited," he replied after taking a sip of Kool-Aid.

"Hello, doctor my son just had some chest pains."

"Is he okay?" the doctor questioned. "How often does he get that pain? I mean, is this the first time?"

"Son was this the first time you had such pain," Asked Mr. Johnson?

"Yeah."

"This was his first time, doctor."

"Let's hope that it's the only time," Mrs. Johnson said, turning to Mr. Johnson as she overheard him.

"Tell your son to calm down, because his heart is still trying to gain strength. And Mr. Johnson, please don't hesitate to come and see me if this happens again."

"Okay doctor. You know, I hope you take care of that issue so we can just move on."

"Don't worry. I have a plan. Remember, she's on drugs. In fact, I have to go and meet her downstairs in the file room. Let me get on with my plan. I will talk to you real soon, I am sure."

Chapter 15

She Doesn't Do Drugs

Two shifts later, Pat's friend and co-worker, Janice, arrived at work in the hospital. "Hey, what's up? " said Janice to the man whose shift was ending.

"Hey, have you heard from your girlfriend, Pat, " he responded.

"No. What's going on?"

"Well, I heard she made up some lie about going to get a file and never came back."

"Oh, really? That doesn't sound like her."

"Well, she did, and I am sure she will be getting written up or something. You guys haven't heard anything from her?"

As soon as Janice's co-worker had spoken, Janice saw the emergency staff rush down to the basement.

"Hey! Where's everybody going?" she called out, worried.

"A body was found in the basement," responded

one of the medical staff.

"Is the person dead?" Janice asked.

"I don't know. We are going to see now. A file clerk found her and she just called us. " Another medical staff responded.

The emergency staff arrived downstairs and took their places.

"Is she breathing?" asked one of the nurses. "No, I am afraid not" said doctor. "How long has she been down here?"

"Since last night, around 10:00, " responded a medical staff.

"Oh! That's why she wasn't noticed earlier."

"Look at this!" screamed a nurse as she straightened the arm of the woman lying on the ground.

They all knew the signs. She must have been using drugs. At that moment, Janice walked in and saw Pat lying dead on the floor, looking drugged out.

"Oh, no! " she screamed. "I can't believe she relapsed. We made a pact."

She ran out the door, crying.

"What's going on? " asked the receptionist that Janice was relieving.

"It's Pat. She is dead from an overdose."

"Are you sure?" he asked, placing his hand over his chest.

"Yeah," she replied, moving her head up and down and hugging him for support as she cried.

She wiped some of her tears, stepped back, and said, "Our supervisor said that she was doing so well."

Someone had called the police, and Officer Perkins arrived to investigate the scene and inform the next of kin. Well, it so happened that Pat had given the name of Mr. Smith's mother as her next of kin.

"Hello."

"Hello. Uh ... Mrs. Smith?"

"Yes. This is she."

"Hello, this is Officer Perkins I need you to come down to the hospital.

"What is it this time?"

"Well, Pat put you down as the next of kin. Is anybody there with you?"

"Nobody but my grandson, Fred. Who is this again?" she replied, wondering who had the nerve to ask her such a question.

"This is the Barry Police Department. My name is Officer Perkins. I need you to come to the St. Mills Hospital in Barry as soon as possible."

"Is this about my son again?"

"I don't know ..."

"What you mean you, 'you don't know'?" the grandmother responded, cutting him off.

"Well, how old is that boy, madam?" he asked.

"He's about eight."

"Can you leave him at the house with anyone?" "I told you that nobody was here except him and me, so I will have to bring him."

"Do you have transportation?"

"No I don't drive."

"Okay. A squad car will be there to pick you up shortly."

"Officer, is this about his mother?"

"I don't know. Just get down here and we will go over the details later.

"Is she ...?"

"Ma'am can you just come down here first?"

All right, Lord. Let her be all right?" she said to herself.

"OK, do you still stay at 3718 Lincoln Ave.?

"Yeah I've been here forever."

"Good. I'll send a squad car there soon."

"Sir, what am I going to tell her son here?"

"Tell him you are going to take a ride in your friend's new squad car, and he is welcome to join.

"All right."

Later, a police car pulls up in front of Mrs. Smith home. Before the officer gets out of his car, he notices Mrs. Smith waving her hand to get his attention that they are coming. The officer waves back and gets back in the car. Mrs. Smith and grandson greet the driving officer. "How are you all doing? I am Officer Perkins."

"I just spoke to a Perkins on the phone."

"Oh, that was me; I couldn't find another officer to ride down here to pick you up. So I just came myself."

Grandma Smith nods her head to acknowledge that she understands.

'Wow! I can't believe I am riding in a squad car. " Fred looked around the car.

As he pulled off, the officer questioned Mrs. Smith, who is sitting in the front seat beside him.

"Drugs? She doesn't touch drugs anymore," she responded, looking at him with narrowed eyes.

"'Anymore? When did she quit?" asked the officer.

"She quit when she found out that she was pregnant with my grandson."

"Are you saying you never saw her use drugs or look high since the pregnancy?"

"Neither her nor my son, rest his soul."

"So is he ...?"The cop asked with a raised brow.

"Yep. He's gone to be with the Lord too." "What happened, if you don't mind me asking?"

She gestured to say no.

"He got hit by a car."

"Oh, yeah, I remember that story about the Coupon Man. That's what we called him at the station."

Mrs. Smith, slightly offended, cuts the officer a mean look.

"But we later called him Mr. Smith, when we found out his real name," he quickly added.

"You know he had those coupons because he was going to take his son to McDonald's and the movies. My grandson told Pat that he'd given John those coupons so he wouldn't forget that he had to take him to the movies. I thought he'd forgotten, and she did too, but he was at the hospital. I knew I'd raised a better son than that, especially since he had a new job."

At that moment, Fred knocked on the window. "Hey! Excuse me, but is that gun loaded?" he asked while pointing at the shot gun between the seats.

"No. I only load it when I have to use it to catch the bad guy. So stay seated and enjoy the ride," said the policeman.

Fred sat back and waved at people as they drove by.

"Where was his new job? " asked the policeman, in his attempt to continue the conversation.

"At that dirty plant downtown," Grandma replied while pointing towards the east, where downtown was located.

"Have you ever been there?"

"No. But Pat, my son's mother went there before she came to work yesterday."

"For what?" Officer Perkins asked.

"My son's boss called and told me that John had left his wallet and stuff there. Pat picked up his clothes and later told me on the phone that she wanted to look for his wallet to see if he had signed to be a donor, because if he hadn't, all hell was going to break loose," she said.

"Can you tell me what she meant by all hell was going to break loose?"

"I was going to ask her today when she got home from work. But she called and told me that he wasn't a donor. She said that she confronted the doctor who did the operation on him. She kept saying that something wasn't right. Then she got a call on another line and had to go and get a file or something downstairs in that dark file room. She hates going there. That was the last time I heard from her."

The officer had a feeling that something was going on and pondered the story.

He pulled up at the hospital.

"Hey! Doesn't my mother work here?" asked Fred.

"Yes, honey, that's right."

"Are we picking her up?"

"Probably, if she's ready."

"Good! I can't wait until I tell her I rode in a police car."

When they entered the hospital, Perkins went to see one of the doctors while the boy and his grandmother waited in the waiting room.

"Is my mother back there?" asked Fred.

The receptionist recognized him from the pictures Pat always carried in her wallet. The receptionist looks away and pretends she is very busy with paperwork.

"Excuse me, excuse me, " Fred shouted trying to get her attention.

The receptionist looked at the grandmother. Mrs. Smith motioned her lips, 'Don't tell him' as she stood behind her grandson.

At that moment, the officer came in along with the doctor.

"Can you take the boy to get a soda?" the doctor asked the receptionist.

"I didn't ask for a soda." Fred said while being escorted to the lobby where the soda machines are located.

As they walked out of Fred's earshot, the doctor introduced himself to Fred's grandmother.

"Hi! My name is Dr. Harvey. And you are ...?"

"I am like Pat's mother."

"Like her mother?" The doctor looked at the policeman.

"Yeah. She's the grandmother of Pat's son. " He replied while pointing in the direction her son was walking. "That's close enough, isn't it?"

"I guess so, if that's all she's got here. We can talk in my office."

"Won't you have a seat?" the doctor asked when they arrived at his office. "Now, she had some very strong mixes of drugs in her body. The mix of drugs caused her heart to go into cardiac arrest, so we lost her. Do you know if she used drugs often?"

"No. She stopped using drugs," Mrs. Smith responded.

"Was something going on in her life that would have made her relapse," asked the doctor?

"Well, yeah. Her boyfriend just died, but she didn't give us any signs that she was that depressed about his death."

"They normally don't," responded the doctor, looking remorseful.

A silent pause filled the room.

"Doctor, who did a heart transplant the other day? " asked the officer breaking the silence.

"Oh, you are talking about Dr. Cashion. I heard he did a very good job of finding a heart. That was a very lucky boy."

"Is he here?"

"No, not yet. He should be here in the next two to three hours. Why, do you ask?"

"Because Mrs. Smith said that he was the last person that Pat talked to. The heart donor was Mrs. Smith's son and he was Pat's boyfriend."

"Oh, really?"

"Speaking of the donor, Officer Perkins," said Mrs. Smith acknowledging something that just came to her head, "there's another thing. Pat was going to tell me something, but she had to go. I believe it was something about John not being a signed donor. She was saying something fishy was going on. " Mrs. Smith said, while staring into space.

"Doctor thank you for your time. I'm going to take Mr. Smith and her grandson home now, " said Officer Perkins.

"Sure, but, can I speak to you, in private?" Dr. Harvey said with a raised brow to Officer Perkins.

"Mrs. Smith, go get Fred and I'll meet you in a minute."

"Thanks again doctor," replied Mrs. Smith as she walked in the direction towards her grandson.

"You know, it was kind of strange, but two of his nurses quit for no apparent reason," said the doctor.

"I am going to contact the detective. This sounds suspicious," replied Officer Perkins.

Chapter 16

The Detective Investigates

When the detective heard the news, he rushed to the hospital. He wanted to reach the doctor's office before anyone else did. He stopped at the help desk for directions.

"Good evening. Where is Dr. Cashion's office?"

"Upstairs, to your left, first door on the right," the receptionist said, pointing up to the left. While she watched the detective go upstairs, she thought, *Pat said that something was fishy about that doctor.*

When the detective looked in the office door, he saw the doctor talking with another man.

"Excuse me. Are you Dr. Cashion?" asked the detective.

"Yes. That's me."

"Can I see you? I want to ask you a couple of questions."

"Okay. Let me finish talking to my friend and I will be right with you."

Dr. Cashion looked at Mr. Johnson as if to say 'what now?' The detective and Mr. Johnson stared deeply at each other as he walked out the office.

"Detective, I will see you now, " the doctor said. "Have a seat."

As he sat down, he noticed a folder on the desk with the victim's name on it. He didn't say anything for now.

"Well, Doc. I bet you are wondering why I am here to talk to you."

"It's not just to talk," the doctor replied, cracking a smile.

"Well, I'll get right to the point. I know your time is valuable," he responded without responding to his joke.

"Yes, " the doctor replied, looking at his watch.

"Do you know a Patricia Dorsey?"

"Yes. She was the receptionist at the front desk."

"Yes, you heard what happened."

"Yes, you know rumors travel around the hospital fast."

He nods his head in agreement.

"When was the last time you saw her?"

"I believe yesterday. I am not a suspect, am I?"

"Why do you say that?"

"I mean, you come here talking to me! What about everybody else? Besides, wasn't she on drugs, already?"

"How did you know that?"

The doctor glanced at her personnel folder on the desk. He started putting stuff away on his desk and grabbed her folder.

"Was that her folder?"

"No this is another patient with the same name."

"Well, Doc, here's my card. Please get back with me if anything comes up. " He laid the card on the corner of the desk.

"Hey, Detective! The doctor yelled while he was in the entrance of the door. Why do you think foul play was involved? How come you just won't take the doctor's word for it, that it was a drug overdose?"

"I have my reasons," the detective replied, narrowing his eyes. "Good bye!"

As he walked out of the office, he realized that he had never told the doctor how Pat died. That raised his suspicions all the way up. On the way downstairs, he decided to stop and talk to Janice, the receptionist.

"Excuse me. Do you know Patricia Dorsey?" asked the detective.

"Yes, and I am still upset by that."

"Yeah, was she a friend of yours?"

"Yeah, she was a good friend," she replied with watery eyes.

"So, first of all sorry for your loss, but can you tell me what happened that night?"

"Well, that night, I heard she went to go get a file and never came back. They say she may have overdosed. You know, she didn't tell me that she was having any urges. We'd made a pact with each other to let each other know when we get an urge. Drugs were the furthest thing from her mind. She'd enrolled in some classes to become a nurse. Pat was looking forward to the future for her and her child. Her boyfriend did just die from a car accident, but I still didn't see drugs in the picture. She was more concerned with what had happened in his death. Apparently, she felt that something fishy was going on. Now, I am starting to feel the same way."

"Okay, I need to talk to some other people. I will get back with you soon."

The detective handed her his card and walked back upstairs to the doctor's office to see if he was available to answer more questions. The office door was opened slightly, so he knocked softly.

"Come in! " shouted the doctor.

The detective walked in and the doctor looked up.

"Oh! It's you. How can I help you again?" he responded irritated.

"Well, I just have a couple more questions." At that moment, the phone rang and the doctor answered.

"Dr. Cashion's office." he answered.

"Hello. This is the operator. You know that boy who you operated on the other day? Isn't his last name something like Johnson?"

"Yeah. Why? What's up?"

"I believe he is on his way back in."

"Okay. Well, let me get prepared for him."

While the doctor was on the phone, the detective noticed Patricia Dorsey's personnel folder on the desk again. He ignored it, again, for now.

"So, what's wrong?"

"I have to go and take care of a transplant patient."

"Is it the transplant you did for the Johnson's son?"

"Yes, and it was successful."

"Successful for who? You or the guy who wasn't a donor? According to some of your staff, Patricia figured that there was more to this donor business than meets the eye. And I am starting to feel the same way."

The doctor gave the detective a deep stare.

"Officer, the next time you come to see me, please bring my lawyer with you. Now, I've got to go and see what is going on with my patient," responded the doctor as he scooted the detective out of the office and ahead of him so he could lock his door.

"I will be seeing you, " said the detective. He moved his arm swiftly upwards, because the doctor had just invaded his space.

The doctor didn't bother to reply. He just ran to the emergency room.

Chapter 17

Mommy, My Chest Hurts

The Johnson's son had come home complaining about chest pains following a playful walk from school. He entered the house breathing hard, and he saw his mother.

"Mom, my chest hurts again," he said, holding his chest. Then he hit the ground.

"Ahhing! Ahhing! Ahhing! " Mrs. Johnson screamed as she grabbed him to make sure he was okay.

"Are you okay? Are you okay!" she hollered.

He lay there, barely breathing.

"Baby, please don't do this now, " she said to herself as she checked his pulse. A moment later, she called 911.

When the ambulance arrived, she was still holding her son. The paramedics asked her to move and tried to resuscitate him. They tried to keep him alive on the way to the hospital, but they did not succeed. When the boy's dad arrived back at the hospital and found out the bad news that his son had died, he was very upset.

"What happened?" Mr. Johnson asked. "He was complaining about chest pains and fell out. I told you to stop trying to fix everything! Fix this and bring me my son back," Mrs. Johnson replied getting up and turning her back to Mr. Johnson.

Mr. Johnson looked down in sorrow.

"What happened?" Mr. Johnson asked the doctor in stride to the room.

"Apparently, the heart couldn't take being a kid again. The rapid movement sent it into cardiac arrest. I am so sorry, but this time, he didn't make it."

"NO! " screamed Mrs. Johnson.

Chapter 18

Mr. Fix-it

Mr. Johnson and his wife were returning home from the hospital. Mrs. Johnson stared at Mr. Johnson.

"How are you going to fix this? Let's see! Can you bring our son back?"

The ride was totally quiet the rest of the way home. When they arrived home, Mrs. Johnson slammed her purse down, and before she could run upstairs, Mr. Johnson grabbed her by the arm.

"Everything is going to be all right. I will fix this," Mr. Johnson said, looking deeply in her eyes.

Mrs. Johnson pulled away, gave him an angry stare, and ran upstairs, crying. Mr. Johnson cursed to himself, threw his keys on the glass coffee table, and broke the glass. Then, he sat on the sofa and started to think about how everything he tries to fix backfires on him later. Like the day he married his wife, Mrs. Johnson.

It had been cloudy all day, and Mrs. Johnson

was very concerned that it might rain. She kept looking out the window of the cabin, because she had hoped to have her wedding at a beautiful resort. Eventually, the sun came out and stayed out, and the wedding appeared to be safe. It appeared to be safe until one bridesmaid screamed out that she had forgotten her shoes.

"I can't believe this. I forgot my shoes!" she shouted.

The maid of honor looked at her and shook her head in disgust. "I felt that somebody would leave something important. Come with me, girl. Your uncle is acting as the gofer for the wedding, and he will take you back to get your shoes."

"I knew that I picked the right bridesmaid. Whose idea was that, anyway?" asked Mrs. Johnson.

"It was actually your man, " said the made of honor.

"I should have known that Mr. Fix-it would have his two cents in it."

Meanwhile, Mr. Johnson and his crew were sitting around on the other side of the cabin, trying to get over their hangovers from the night before.

"Here! Try this," one of the groomsmen said as he handed Mr. Johnson a bread stick.

"You are giving me a dry piece of bread? It's too late for bread. I should have had some bread last night."

"Yeah, bread can't help him now. But here!"

said the best man, handing him a banana.

"What the hell is this going to do? " Mr. Johnson asked. "Here! Give me your bread, too. I will try anything now."

One of the groomsmen handed him a pitcher of water to try to get him to flush the drunkenness out of his system. He took a cup of water and started drinking. Then, there was a knock at the door. It was the bridesmaid.

"Hey! I am going to dash back home. I left my shoes, and I was wondering if anyone needed to go back for something or would like me to bring anything."

"Yeah, can you go to the store and get me a new head?" Mr. Johnson said, holding his head.

"Boy! You mean to tell me you got so drunk that you didn't think about having a hangover today."

"Please don't tell my baby."

"Boy! I am not going to mess up her day. Just make sure you take care of your illness before the wedding starts. So anyway, do you need anything or what?"

They all shook their heads to say no. As she was leaving, the pastor walked in.

"Hello everyone." The men looked around the room to make sure that nothing was there that would disgust the pastor. "So, how was the party last night?"

"Party?" said the best man. "We didn't have any party."

"Now, you know that it's not good to lie to a pastor," said the pastor, looking at him with a raised brow.

"Okay, we may have had a little something." "I can tell by looking in the groom's eyes."

"Oh, yeah! That's what I need. Can somebody catch her and tell her I need a bottle of visine?"

Before anyone could get up and try to catch her, the pastor stopped them.

"Oh, don't worry. I've got to go back out to get some things, so I will stop by the store and pick you up a bottle."

"Thank you, pastor, but are you sure? Because I am sure the limo driver isn't doing anything."

"Yes, I am sure. In the meantime, I know it's kind of late, but here are the vows I am going to read for you to repeat. Look this over and inform me if you need to leave anything out."

"Yes, everything. But do I take her and does she take me? I need to get this over with so I can go to sleep and get rid of this headache," Mr. Johnson said as he put his hand on his head again.

"Here's a pencil. Let me know. I will talk to you guys later. God bless you."

The pastor left and Mr. Johnson read the material. Meanwhile, the bridesmaids were in the other room, discussing the wedding.

"You know, I really like your wedding. The location and the decoration is just nice. This has to have cost a fortune," said one of the bridesmaids.

"I think they got scholarships," said another bridesmaid with a smile.

"For real," the first girl replied.

"Girl, no! I was just kidding. Hell! I wish you could get a student loan for a wedding. Hell! Everybody's wedding would be tight."

"Hell yeah!" they all responded and give each other high-fives.

"My baby hooked this up, and I really don't know how much everything cost, but I love the location," Mrs. Johnson said.

"You mean to tell me that you didn't have no say so about this either? I mean he is always in control," said one of the girls.

"Well, he told me where he wanted to have it, and I remember saying, 'Yeah, that is a nice place to get married.' The next thing I knew, he had all this fixed in a week. I believe that's why I am not tripping on my day — because it is not mine or I had nothing to with this, anyway. But I admit, I love it and this is my day to shine and I plan to do just that."

"This is very nice. It's too bad I can't copy it whenever I get married," said another bridesmaid.

"Girl, this land may be a graveyard by that time," one of the girls said. She laughed, and so did all the other bridesmaids.

At the same time, the sounds of an ambulance blared in the background. In the other room, Mr. Johnson was still complaining about his headache.

"Please come and get me!" he said when he heard the ambulance. "I am right here with a splitting headache."

All his friends laughed and continued to offer him things to get rid of his headache. Then, there was a knock at the door. The door opened and standing there was the maid of honor who left her shoes. She looked worried.

"Doesn't the pastor drive a green Cadillac with the word pastor on the license plate?"

"Yeah," said Mr. Johnson.

"I think I just seen him in a bad accident. I sent one of your groomsmen to find out if it was him and to make sure he was all right."

"You know you can't tell the bride this news. I will take care of this before it gets out of hand," Mr. Johnson said with a blank stare.

Moments later, the groomsman returned.

"I've got some good news and some bad news. The good news is that he is going to be all right. The bad news is that he hit his head hard. He is in and out of consciousness, and he will not be able to do the wedding."

Everyone glanced at the groom and put their head down.

"Hey! This wedding is in one hour. I am going to need another preacher." He looked around the room. "Donald, didn't you tell me you teach Sunday School sometimes?" the groom asked one of his men.

"Man, I am not ordained," replied Donald.

"It doesn't matter. All you got to do is read this stuff the pastor just gave me and you are done. Come on. There will be a pretty cent in it for you."

"Man, you don't have to pay me —I mean, yes you do! " he said quickly with a smile. "Give me that!"

He took the material to the corner to read it to himself.

"Good idea! Now that that is taken care of, whose idea was it to get me drunk last night?"

They all pointed to the best man.

"Well, you are coming down twice to escort Donald's bridesmaid."

The best man smiled in agreement.

Meanwhile, they were able to keep all the problems a secret from the bride. The only other person who knew something was the maid of honor, and she wasn't going to upset the bride.

The wedding went according to schedule, and Mrs. Johnson figured everything was all right.

Mr. Johnson was distracted by the noise Mrs. Johnson made when she walked back into the room. She saw her husband sitting down and looking sad beside the glass coffee table he broke with his keys.

"Honey, how did —? " She stopped to take a breath. "Oh, forget it. I am sorry for telling you off on the way home from the hospital. Will you forgive me? I am sure this is as hard for you as it is for me."

Chapter 19

The Funerals

"I know that the question you are asking is" 'Why?' said the pastor in his closing remarks. "Why this child, who did no one harm? Why did he have to go so soon? These are questions that only God knows the answers to, so please don't blame yourself or feel that you could have prevented this. There was nothing that you could have done, that I could have done, or that anybody could have done. In God's eyes, he had just finished his position here at this time. Please don't believe that anyone can fix this. It had to happen. Amen."

While the preacher was talking, Mr. Johnson subconsciously looked to see who was present to show his last respects to his boy. He noticed cousins from all over. He noticed some school teachers, students, and to his surprise, some hospital staff. He smiled a little as he took his seat and continued to console his wife by putting his arm around her shoulders.

"Ashes to ashes. Dust to dust ... " The preacher continued his closing remarks.

Mr. Johnson was distracted when he heard another funeral party enters the cemetery. From a distance, he noticed a little boy getting out of a limousine with a woman who Mr. Johnson thought must be his mother or grandmother. The boy looked like he was the same age as his son would have been. Then he noticed someone's hand extended for him to shake. He got up to hug the person. However, Mrs. Johnson never got up. She just sat there while people bent down to hug her.

Meanwhile, the funeral party that Mr. Johnson noticed was Pat's, Mr. Smith's Girlfriend. The boy and the lady he noticed were Fred and his grandmother Ms. Smith. After the funeral, Grandma Smith decided to have a small reception at her home. During the reception, Grandma went around the room asking for kin Fred and then if they can take care of him. No one was willing, and she became worried about her grandson. She knew that she wouldn't be able to take care of him.

About an hour later, the people started leaving Grandma's house. The last person left and she realized she had no one to turn too. She sat at dining table watching Fred watch television and wondered what she should do. Since her son died she been considering moving into a senior citizen home. This is because she knew without the help of her son around the house; the value of her house will go down dramatically. Unfortunately, the senior home prohibits children staying at the home. Grandma sighs as she takes another look at Fred on the couch. "What can I do? Lord, what can I do?" she cried as she closes her eyes hoping to get an answer from God. After 30 seconds go by, she lets out some wind before calling Fred.

"Fred can you come here?"

"Yes ma'am." Fred said in stride coming to see what she wants.

When Fred comes in front of his Grandma, she wastes no time in getting to the point.

"Fred, do you know of any relatives on your father's side that wouldn't mined taking care of you?"

"No. " Fred swallows. "I thought you were going to take care of me. " He added.

Grandma Smith takes in some wind before speaking again. "Well Fred, you know I am old and I wouldn't be able to give you the proper parenting as someone who is much younger will. Besides, I am planning on moving out of this house because I can't keep up with the maintenance. So again, is there anyone you can think of that may be interested in taking care of you? Anyone? She asked looking directly in Fred's eyes.

Fred looks down, then back up. "Grandma, I lost my mom and dad and you too. "How come this is happening to me? Am I cursed?" Fred asked looking back and folding his arms.

"No, Jesus loves you. I do too. That's why I am not going to even try to mess up your life and say I can take care of you, knowing I can't." She puts one hand on Fred's shoulders and slightly pinches it while giving him a helpless look. "Everything is going to be alright, alright." She adds as Fred slowly lifts his head up establishing eye contact with her.

"Let me go! " Fred yelled as he moves her hand away from his shoulders and quickly turns around and storms to his room. "Jesus don't love me! " he screams as he continues to storm to his bedroom.

"Yes He does." She said. "Yes He does." Grandma repeated this time looking up in the air for reassurance.

Chapter 20

The Detective Collects More Evidence

The detective went to talk to one of the two nurses who had quit around the time of Mr. Smith's death.

"How often did you work with Dr. Cashion?" he asked.

"All the time, or at least every day that I went to work. I used to be his favorite."

"So, where were you on the day of Patricia Dorsey's death?"

"Oh, this is about the receptionist." The nurse frowned.

"Yeah, what did you think it was for? " the detective asked.

"Nothing, I thought it was about something else. Please stay focused on the receptionist's death. She seemed to be a nice person."

"Did you know her?"

"No not really but I'd seen her around, and I met her once when ... never mind."

"No, I would like to know whatever you got to say. I don't know if you know it or not, but if you withhold information, I can hold you for obstructing an investigation."

"I was just referring to the time when she tried to come into a room when she heard a heart monitor go off. Well, she didn't know it, but we were preparing for a heart transplant."

"For who?"

"Well..." she hesitated and avoided looking the detective in the eye. "We didn't know his name. We just called him John Doe."

The detective looked at her as if she was keeping some information from him.

"Well, he looked like he was straight up off the streets," she continued.

"So y'all just took his heart, right?"

"Hey! We were talking about the receptionist here, right?" she asked to change the subject. He raised his eyebrow.

"Now, like I said," the nurse continued, "she appeared to be a nice person, because I asked her to take the heart down to the fourth floor, and she did it without any problems. Anybody else would have told me to do it myself."

"Why didn't you do it yourself?" the detective asked, shrugging his shoulders.

"Because I needed to be with the doctor."

The detective gave her his card and thanked her for her help. Then he went to meet Janice at the hospital. She arrived and found him waiting for her.

"Hi. I guess you know I have to start work in fifteen minutes," said Janice after a sigh when she sees the detective waiting for her.

"So, do you know why I am here again?"

"Yes. I assume it's to talk about my friend." "You know, there is something fishy about the doctor here."

"Who, Dr. Cashion?"

"Yeah, what made you think I was talking about him? " he asked realizing that everybody must feel the same way about the doctor.

"Because, I think I told you before that Pat had been talking the same way."

"Right," he responded nodding his head in agreement.

"Yeah, she had some questions concerning whether her boyfriend was a donor or not. I believe that earlier, she had told me that she had carried a heart to the lab. Later, she realized that she had been carrying her boyfriend's heart."

"Do you remember what day that was?"

"Yeah, it was like three or four weeks ago. My log will show the records."

"Do you remember his name?"

"Yeah, she talked about him a lot, but he didn't have any ID when he came in. We all figured that he was off the streets. His name was John — John Smith, I believe."

"Did you ever meet him? " he asked as he turned the paper on his note pad.

"Well, no."

"Okay. Let's go back to this drug thing. You said before that Pat wasn't into drugs anymore, right?"

"Right and I recently ran into Ted. " She put her hand over her mouth as if she was supposed to keep his name a secret. "Anyway, he would have let me know if she was back getting hits."

"Did you say Ted?"

She looked down.

The detective knew this guy and he happened to owe him a favor.

"Thank you. That will be enough for today," the detective responded as he closed his notepad.

Chapter 21

I Need a Favor

Ted's beeper goes off. "Somebody called?" Ted asked when he returned the call. "Yeah. This is Detective Mac."

"What's up? What's up with you?"

"Are you selling crooked stuff in my neighborhood?"

"Ah no, don't even try it. I already heard she OD'd. Who was she, anyway?"

"Her name was Pat —Patricia Dorsey to be exact."

"Oh no! That was my boy's girl."

"So you knew her?"

"She used to be a customer of mine, but I haven't seen her since she went to rehab and got a job. No, I take that back. She and John were trying to buy some drugs one day. I don't know what was going on, because later, I found my drugs on the street where they had bought them. You know, I really liked it when she and my boy hooked up, rest his soul. That's a coincidence isn't it? I will be over to talk to their son and show my condolences. How is he taking everything?"

"I don't know, but he has been placed where he can get help."

"What do you mean?"

"He is in one of those homes?"

"What about Mrs. Smith?"

"Well, I heard that she moved to a senior home."

"Straight. Well what home is the boy in?"

"I can't share that information." The detective looked at the clock on the wall and realized that he was running late for a meeting. "I will beep you later, all right?" he said as he pushed his seat back to stand up.

Before he hung up, Ted asked him a question. "How is the job going, Mac?"

"All right."

"Do you remember telling me that if I tell you what's going on in the streets, you will let me go and never arrest me again? Since you just got the position, I thought I would help a brother out."

"Help me out! The nerve! Anyway, I was just going to say that if you remember anything strange happening that day, give me a call."

"As a matter of fact, I don't know, but a doctor from the suburbs did call me to get something from me that day. He was acting really strange."

"Was it Dr. Cashion?"

Wow! You are good! Ted thought, but he didn't answer.

"Was it him? " the detective said, noticing the silence.

"I don't want to give you everything."

The detective reached for the arm of his seat to sit back down to listen closely.

"Well, did this doctor say what he wanted?"

"Uh ... yeah."

"Did you deliver?"

"Well, what do you think? Anyway, he also told me that he was working on a plan."

"Hey Ted! You really helped me. I knew I wasn't making a mistake when we made that agreement."

"This really doesn't have anything to do with you. But it has a lot to do with my friend John. We made an agreement back in the old days that I would be there for him in anyway I could. But speaking of our agreement, how long must I be under it?"

"As long as you are selling drugs."

"Whatever! Peace out, detective. I got another call coming in, " Ted replied as he glanced at his caller ID.

"All right, I will be in touch."

"I know."

As they hung up, they both thought about the day they made their agreement.

Chapter 22

If You Do This, Then ...

Before the detective became a detective, he was a police officer, of course. Mac was in charge of the officers on the night shift. One day, he arrived at work, clocked in, and noticed a memo that said the department was seeking new detectives. Since childhood, he had always wanted to be a police officer. It all started when he watched an episode of *Cops* and noticed how the cops kept the peace. He really showed an interest when the cops arrested those who were responsible for domestic violence. There was something about misusing a woman that he disliked immensely. When he graduated from high school, he studied at college and majored in criminal justice. After graduating with a bachelor's degree, he went straight into the force.

When he saw the memo, he decided to apply for the detective position, and before he knew it, he was a top contender. He had been on the force for five years and had a record of nearly perfect attendance. The force requested that he go through a one-year probation period. That year seemed like a decade. He worked hard to keep his position, because he was not at all interested in going back to the uniform. He wanted to make sure that didn't happen.

One day, Detective Mac and his partner got a call about possible drug trafficking in the city. The person they were to look for might be a witness in one of the open cases. The men hopped in the squad car and drove off without turning on their siren. When they arrived at the location, five individuals were standing on the sidewalk. One of them turned around and looked at the car and the people inside.

"A man 5-0! " he yelled when he recognized them.

They all scattered, but Mac and his partner jumped out the car, ran and caught two of them. They were lucky because his partner caught the very person they were looking for.

"Detective, I got my man, so you can let that one go, " his partner said.

Just as he was about to let him go, he noticed a bulge in his pocket.

"Hey! What's this?" he asked as he reached into the man's pocket.

The drug dealer tried to resist, but the cop pulled out the drugs.

"Wow! What's this?" the detective asked again as he looked at the drugs in one hand and held the dealer with the other.

"What you got there?" asked his partner.

"Nothing. It's nothing," said Detective Mac, with a smirk at the drug dealer.

"All right. Well, let him go so we can take this one back to the station and tell the sergeant we got our man."

"All right."

Then, Detective Mac said quietly to his man, "Hey, I am new on the force and I need somebody to inform me about what's going on in the streets. I will let you go if you give me your word that you will help me sometimes. This is between me and you only. You got my word."

"What's a cop's word?"

"The only word you got. I'll be seeing you around."

They went their opposite ways.

When the detective got back in the car, his partner looked at him and asked, "Did you know him? What were y'all doing? Catching up on old times?"

"I know him from around. He just tries to be hard sometimes. But he is cool."

"Okay, whatever. You know, I believe he is starting to sell. To be honest, I thought you'd caught something on him."

"No, it was a false alarm," replied Detective Mac.

The other detective gave Detective Mac a quick incredulous stare and it forced him to look the other way. They made their way back to the station.

That was several years ago. On this day, like that day, Mac arrived back at the station. He would match the evidence that Ted had just given him about Dr. Cashion with the other information he had collected. Meanwhile, Ted hung up the phone and looked in the telephone directory to find which foster home Mr. Smith's son, Fred, was in. Then, he went out to answer the call that had interrupted his conversation with the detective.

Chapter 23

Foster Kid

Mr. Johnson sat on the couch reading the newspaper, trying to put his mind on things besides his now deceased son. He ran across an ad from an adoptive agency. It said three kids needed a home. This gave him the idea that he could get another son. He couldn't imagine his wife bearing another child, especially after the painful birth she had experienced of her first and only child. Besides, Mr. Johnson wasn't ready to go through the hassle of having a baby in the house. He would try to find a child the same age as his deceased son. Instead of consulting with his wife first, Mr. Fix-it went to the adoption agency himself to ask some questions and check out the prospects. He and a social worker stood outside, looking at the listed prospects, as they carried on a conversation.

"So, why do you want to adopt?" the social worker asked, giving him a deep stare.

"My wife and I have been thinking about this for a while."

"Okay, but what brought the conversation up about adoption."

"Why all the questions?" Mr. Johnson grew angry. "You act like these kids don't need anyone!"

A ball bounced off the window and a boy wearing a red jacket caught it. Mr. Johnson looked directly at the boy's eyes.

"Well, it's like this. My son just passed."

"Oh, I am so sorry for that." The social worker put his pen down to make sure Mr. Johnson knew he had his undivided attention. "So, you guys aren't looking for a replacement for your son, are you?"

"No! I just thought it would be a good surprise for my wife."

"You can't surprise your wife with a human being. A human being is not a dog. "To be honest, did you even discuss this matter with your wife first?"

"For what?" Mr. Johnson sat back in the chair. "She will be so happy when she sees that I brought her a new son."

"Mr. Johnson, I am just trying to protect the child. Besides, there is a lot of paperwork you must complete that will need both your signatures."

"Okay, I will talk to her. But before I go, tell me about that child." He pointed at the child in the red jacket.

"He just came in last month, and so far, he appears to be a good kid."

"What's his name? How old is he?"

"I think his name is Fred. He is about ten or eleven years old."

"That would be perfect! That's about the same age that my son was. " Mr. Johnson gleamed.

"Don't you think you guys need to take some time off from having a child so you have a chance to exhale?"

"I think we need this change to keep our minds off our son."

"It would probably be a good thing for him to be adopted before he gets corrupted by being in the system. Here! Do me a favor. Go and talk this over with your wife. Then get back with me."

Chapter 24

Baby, Why Not?

Mr. Johnson walked home after visiting the residential home. He saw his wife in the kitchen preparing supper.

"Honey, can I talk to you? " Mr. Johnson asked.

"Yes, what do you need?"

"Are you still mad at me?"

"Baby, no. You didn't do anything to me. I understand that you did what you thought was right. And I can't really say that I didn't know what you were up too. I just knew you were up to being Mr. Fix-it."

"Well, honey, I am fixing it again."

"If you can't bring our son back, then you aren't fixing anything."

"No, but how about a replacement?"

"A replacement? No one will ever replace my son."

"Yeah, I know but—"

Mrs. Johnson cut in before he could finish. "But

nothing! What you got up your sleeve, anyway?"

"Have you ever thought about adoption?"

"You mean to tell me that you are already thinking about that kind of stuff and our son hasn't even set in the dirt yet! Honey, you can't replace your son."

"I was just thinking that it would get us thinking about other things instead of our son. And I saw a boy at the adoption agency. He is about our son's age, and he needs a new home."

"Suppose the parents come back like in a movie I once saw."

"This is not the movies. Plus I am sure the social worker would have told me if he wasn't totally available."

"Poor child! Did you see him?"

"Yes I saw him and I would like you to see him too, before we meet him."

"Let me think about it. " She sighed. "You know that if I see him, my heart is going to melt."

"Well, the appointment is set for tomorrow afternoon at 4:30."

"What? You already made an appointment?"
Silence filled the room and lasted a full thirty seconds. Mr. Johnson waited anxiously.

"Well, I guess since you went to all that trouble ... Why not?"

"I knew you would see things my way, " Mr. Johnson responded while giving her a hug.

The next day, Mrs. Johnson waited for Mr.

Johnson to finish work. He returned home with a toy to give to the little boy when they meet him.

"Hi baby! I am home," he sang.

"What's that, Ricky Ricardo?" Mrs. Johnson asked, cracking a smile and pointing at the bag.

"Very funny!" He smiled and assumed that she was in a better mood. "This is a toy to give to our new boy."

"What? Is he going to be a new puppy or something?"

Mr. Johnson looks at her with a partial smile. "But I've been thinking ... " Mrs. Johnson continued.

Mr. Johnson cut her off before she could finish. "Well, I hope you've been doing something while you were here all day!"

He smiled, but Mrs. Johnson didn't.

"Anyway ... " She started again while walking to get her coat from the closet.

"Honey, I don't want to be late," said Mr. Johnson, cutting her off again. "We will talk about what you've been thinking on the way to the place."

Mr. Johnson walked into the front room to check the caller ID. As they walked out to the car, Mr. Johnson asked Mrs. Johnson a question.

"So who called from the police station?"

"Oh yeah! That's what got me thinking. A detective called and — Wait a minute! Are you snooping around the caller ID again?" She stopped talking and gave a penetrating stare. Then she continued. "Well, anyway, the detective called while you were at work to ask me some questions about Dr. Cashion."

"You didn't tell him anything, right?"

He took his eyes off the road for a moment to look at her. Then he quickly slammed the breaks to avoid hitting the car in front of him, which had slowed down at just that moment.

"No! And keep your eyes on the road!" shouted Mrs. Johnson. "I told the detective that you had been the one dealing with him most of the time. Also, that you are the only one who will talk to him about that. Then he yelled that our son's donor had a ten-year-old son. I hung up the phone after that and didn't pick it up when he called back. So anyway, this is what I've been thinking about. How old is the boy at the foster home?"

"He is around the same age."

"Are we going to find out what happened to his parents?"

"No, honey. That's just a coincidence, and we are not going to bring that up when we get to the adoption home!"

Deep inside, Mr. Johnson felt that the similarities were obvious, but he really wanted another boy. Mrs. Johnson figured that if this was Mr. Smith's son, they owed him this favor anyway.

Chapter 25

Mrs. Johnson Meets Fred

Mr. And Mrs. Johnson arrived at the adoption home and were greeted by the social worker.

"Hello, Mr. Wally. This is my wife, Mrs. Johnson."

"You can call me Phil. Hello Mrs. Johnson. I hope your husband told you why you are here."

"Yes. Where is the boy?"

"Wait! Wait! Come in and have a seat. Let me tell you how this is going to work. The kids are about to have lunch —I mean dinner —in a minute. We will sit down and watch them interact, and then you can tell me if this is the kind of child you want to deal with. I must remind you that all the kids here have behavior problems."

They walked into the cafeteria, sat at the supervisors' table, ordered coffee, and waited for the youngsters to come in. The children arrived acting crazy and goofy, but when they saw the visitors, they tried to act civilized and took their seats for dinner.

"Which one is he? " Mrs. Johnson asked.

"I think Mr. Johnson was looking at the one in the red hood," said Phil.

"He had on red the last time I saw him, didn't he? " Mr. Johnson said.

"Yeah, but he's not in a gang if that's what you are thinking. I think red is his favorite color. He wears other colors sometimes."

"He is almost the same height as my son was," Mrs. Johnson said with watery eyes.

"I am sorry. You did say your only son was deceased. Right?" Phil asked.

"Yes and all we had was that one son, " Mr. Johnson replied, putting one finger in the air.

"Honey, hold my hand. Please don't let me start crying," Mrs. Johnson said, looking sad.

"Would you like to meet him? " asked Phil.

Mr. and Mrs. Johnson nodded their heads to say yes.

"Well, don't say anything. I am going to get his attention." He looked towards the children. "Fred! Fred, come here. You got on red again."

"Yes, I told you red is my favorite color," Fred said, holding his jacket and showing that he was proud of it.

"Are you sure you are not in a gang?" Phil asked jokingly.

"No sir. Besides, my daddy gave this jacket to

me, " he responded proudly.

"Suppose someone tried to take it off you. What would you do? " Phil asked to avoid talking about his daddy, afraid that the boy would get emotional.

"This is a free world, and I can wear whatever I want."

Fred made eye contact with Mr. Johnson and looked away.

"Okay. Go back to your place and try not to wear anything red for a week."

"So, I guess you are taking me shopping," Fred replied sarcastically.

They all laughed.

"We will see. I know your allowance will be here soon."

Fred nodded in agreement. Then Fred returned to his table and his friends started laughing.

"You know those people are interested in adopting you, don't you? " said one of the youths at the table.

"Who? Them?" Fred asked and pointed at the table where Mr. and Mrs. Johnson were sitting.

"Yeah. They think we don't know it, but we know that we should be on our best behavior now. Can you imagine how many kids would be out of their seats stealing and hitting if those people weren't here? You will learn that it's all a game, depending on how long you are here."

At the supervisors' table, Mr. and Mrs. Johnson discussed their thoughts about Fred with Phil.

"So, what do you think?" the social worker asked.

Mr. and Mrs. Johnson looked at each other.

"You heard him. What do you think?" Mr. Johnson asked Mrs. Johnson, hoping to get a straight answer.

"I don't know. It may be too soon."

"Well, you guys make up your minds. You are welcome to visit to observe him anytime."

"Cool. But, so there won't be any surprises. What criteria must we follow before we get the child?" Mr. Johnson asked.

"Providing none of the boy's family members shows an interest, you first must come and visit him regularly for a month. Then he can go home with you on weekends for a month. Then you can keep him for a year on probation. So, you guys think about it and come see me when you are ready."

"Has anybody been coming to see him? " asked Mr. Johnson, curiously.

"Oh, yeah. This one guy comes. He called and said that he was a good friend of the family. He was a friend of his dad. I think it's his Godfather. But he had no interest in adopting Fred. We also take him to visit his grandmother, who admitted herself to a nursing home."

"So, what about his biological parents, where are they?" Mrs. Johnson asked, feeling Mr. Johnson's deep stare.

"Oh, I never told you about what happened to his parents, well it's really not good for me to share this information now but it appears that you guys may really adopt him. So, his father died at the hospital after getting hit by a car."

Mrs. Johnson quickly turned her head at Mr. Johnson because her assumption may be right. "And his mother died from a drug overdose." "But his grandmother who signed over the rights is in a retirement home."

"I guess it would be wise to go see her. Right?" said Mr. Johnson.

"I guess," Phil replied as he gathered his papers together. "Well, I have another family coming in to see another child. Here's some paperwork for you all to complete. It's for the state to check whether you have a criminal record. I am sure you are all clear. Right?"

Mrs. Johnson started to think about the detective who had called the house that afternoon.

Chapter 26

Getting Closer to Solving the Case

Dr. Cashion knew that detective Mac was going out of his way to solve this case. He called Mr. Johnson.

"Hello Mr. Johnson. This is Dr. Cashion. I overheard a detective asking my workers questions about both Mr. Smith and Pat Dorsey."

"Oh, no! Can I get in trouble for asking you to do such a thing?"

"Yes, I believe that's called conspiracy."

"You won't tell on me, will you?"

"No, it was all on me."

"Good, because my wife and I want to adopt a new son."

"Already? Wow! " He paused. "Anyway, I've got to go and think of my next move."

"Hey Doc! Remember our agreement?"

"Yeah."

"Well, it still stands. I will be there for you, all right?"

"All right. In the meantime, I've got work to do."

The doctor opened his bag and pulled out some drugs. He saw that he was short, so he decided to call the drug dealer. He punched his number and heard the beep of confirmation. While waiting for the return call, he entertained the idea of having the drug dealer kill the detective. His phone rang.

"Dr. Cashion speaking."

"What's up, doc? You called," Ted responded. "You need something?"

"Yeah, I need some more drugs, but I also need something else."

"What else do you need?"

"Do you know a Detective Mac?"

"Yeah, he tried to bust me a couple of times. As a matter of fact," Then Ted remembered the detective's questions about Dr. Cashion and felt that his cover as an informer might be blown. "Never mind. What's up? What about him?"

"As a matter of fact — what? Has he talked to you, too? " Dr. Cashion asked in an uneasy tone.

"No! No! But I heard he is looking for somebody who may have sold that lady those drugs."

"I got an idea. Can you meet me in about an hour?"

"At the halfway spot in an hour."

The doctor informed the head nurse that he would be out. While driving, he started thinking of how to commit this crime. He arrived at the meeting place and waited for Ted to show up. Finally, he arrived, walked to the passenger side of the doctor's car, and got inside.

"Man, you are late. Anyway, here's what I need you to do."

"Hold up, doc. Let's first do the transaction. Then we can talk. You know I am a businessman first."

Ted reached into his inside jacket pocket and pulled out the drugs. The doctor took the packet and gave Ted the money. The exchange was made clean.

"Now, can we talk?" the doctor asked.

"Cool! What's up? " Ted asked as he put the money in his pocket without counting it.

"Let me get straight to the point."

"Yes, please do. You are on my time," Ted replied cutting him off.

"Well, here it is. How much will it cost me to have you to kill someone?"

"Kill who? The detective? Hey, man! You must be out of your mind. First of all, I am not in the business of killing people. Especially a police officer!"

"I will make it worth your while," the doctor responded with an honest facial expression.

"Man, there would not be enough money in the world for me to kill a police officer unless my life was in danger."

"That's it! We will act as if it was a drug bust gone badly. You've got to do this for me. Otherwise, I will tell the cops that you sell drugs. How does a hundred thousand dollars sound?"

"Are you threatening me? Ted countered. "How about a quarter of a million dollars?"

"What? Okay. I know someone who owes me a favor. In fact, it's his fault I am in this situation."

"In what situation? Why do you need the cop killed anyway?"

"Well, I guess I can share it with you because I know you won't tell the cops since they are already looking for you. Besides, I got some stuff on you as well."

"There you go threatening me again. Doc, what's up? What have you got into?"

"I need a shoulder, and you are about the only person who is lower than I am."

Ted gives him a hard stare as if to say 'whatever'.

"So anyway, one day this man brought his son to the hospital with a bad heart. In fact, it was so bad he needed a replacement. Then this man came in who had been hit by a car. He looked as if he was a bum and had nothing to live for."

"No! You didn't!" Ted responded, and his mouth dropped open with surprise.

"Yes, we did. Then we came to find out he had a son."

The drug dealer started wondering if the doctor

was talking about his friend John.

"Duh! Why are you so quiet?" the doctor asked, noticing the silence.

"It's nothing." Ted was silent for two more seconds. Then he asked, "So what made you do something like that?"

"Well, the man who's going to give me half the money for what you are going to do for me said he would give me a quarter of a million dollars if I would do that for him."

"You killed a guy for a quarter of a million? You are a doctor! You can make that in a year."

"Yes, I am a doctor with a drug habit. Anyway, he was already hurt real bad."

"You don't think he could have made it? " Ted asked, disgusted.

"Yeah, he had a good heart from all that walking, I guess, but I just didn't think anybody cared about him. So I took the quarter of a mil', and now I have to give it to you."

The drug dealer kept his composure, because the similarities between the doctor's victim and his friend might just be a coincidence. Since he was planning to get whoever killed Mr. Smith, he thought he'd keep everything to himself. Then, no one would make any connection to him when it happened. He took a breath and said, "All right. I will do it. When can I get the money?"

"After you commit the crime," the doctor responded.

"All right. But you have to give me at least half in advance."

All right. Mr. Johnson and I will talk about this and I will meet you somewhere soon to give you half.

"Mr. Johnson?"

"Yeah, the other guy who is involved in this."

"Oh. All right. I will see you later."

Chapter 27

In Which Hospital Did He Die?

Ted was visiting his friend's son at the residential home. "Hello. Guess what? We may have a couple to adopt your friend's son, " the Social Worker Phil said cheerfully.

"Already? I thought it would take years before something like that happened," replied Ted.

"Well, this is awkward, but things do happen," said Phil.

"Can Fred and I meet in a private room? I want to talk to him, man to man."

"Yes, but how private do you want it? You will have to keep the door open, but no one will be nearby to hear your conversation. You can take this room right here."

Ted walked into a room that looked like an interrogation room with furniture. He took a seat, and a short while later, Fred walked in, smiling slightly.

"Hey boy! What's going on? How are yah? " Ted asked.

"I am cool. Are you coming to take me out of this place?"

"No, man. You know my situation," Ted replied hitting his chest repeatedly with his opened hand.

"Oh yeah, you are not working now. But you are doing something." Fred looked him up and down then just looked down. "Ain't them gators?" he asked with a hint of sarcasm.

"You know it, " Ted replied proudly. "But let me talk to you about something. First, what hospital did your dad die in?"

"A hospital in the suburbs," he replied, and he pointed north.

"Why was he all the way down there? He worked downtown, right?"

"I don't know. But guess what!"

"What?" Ted responded.

"My grandma told me that he was still living through someone else. He gave his heart away to let someone else live. My grandma said that I should be proud of him for doing that. But my mother acted as if she wasn't proud. All she kept saying was that he wasn't a donor. Even if he wasn't, he still would have done that I think." Fred stops talking for a brief moment as he stares off. Especially, if he was already dead." He adds. I wonder if I am ever going to meet whoever took his heart. I will tell them to be a good person like my daddy."

The drug dealer became upset because he knew his hunch was right. He excused himself and informed Fred that he would come back tomorrow. As he was driving away, he wiped tears from his eyes. At that moment, another car drove past him and they almost hit each other. Mr. Johnson blew his horn in anger.

"Fool! Watch where you are going," he yelled.

Mr. Johnson and Mrs. Johnson parked in the same spot where Ted had been parked. They walked to the front door and rang the doorbell. Phil answered the door.

"Wow! Fred is getting a lot of visitors today."

"Oh yeah? Why do you say that?" asked Mr. Johnson.

"Because his dad's friend just visited, and now you all are here. This is a good day for Fred."

"I wish I had caught him, because I wanted to meet him, " Mrs. Johnson responded looking disappointed.

"I am sure you guys will meet some day soon," said Phil.

Mr. and Mrs. Johnson's visit was good. In fact, it was so good that they made up their minds to adopt Fred as soon as possible.

Chapter 28

Did You Get That Money from That Guy?

Later that day, Dr. Cashion called Mr. Johnson. "Mr. Johnson, can you help me with something?"

"Hey doc! I just had a good visit, and nothing can bring me down. So how can I help you?"

"Well, I need about $250,000 to help me stay out of jail."

"Is that your bond money?" Mr. Johnson asked in disbelief.

"NO! That's my never-see-jail money!"

"Doc, I am so sorry, but things are very tight. I paid you, and now I am paying the lawyer so I can properly adopt a son."

"I didn't want to have to go here, but mister, if you don't do this, I will tell them about what you did to assist with me killing that man."

"Doc, that was your call!"

"Yeah, but it was your suggestion and you knew I did this, so you are just as guilty as I am. This may also shut down your adoption rights."

"Well, I don't want to disappoint my wife. When do you need the money?"

"The sooner the better."

"I will get it as soon as possible. But you've got to promise that I will never hear from you again about this."

"You've got my word." Dr. Cashion's phone clicked. He looked at the caller ID and saw that it was Ted. "Hey, I've got to take a call. You will let me know when you get it, right?"

"Sometime tomorrow — but I will call you," Mr. Johnson responded feeling upset.

The doctor clicked off and took his call.

"Hello."

"Did you get the money from that guy, what'shis-name?"

"What, Mr. Johnson?" the doctor said weakly.

"No, what's his first name? Everybody's last name is Johnson."

"I think Reggie," the doctor replied, wondering why he needed that information.

"Yeah, that's it, " Ted replied as he wrote the name down.

"Well, I was just talking to him. He will call me when he gets his half."

"Come on, now, we don't have a lot of time. They can arrest you so fast when you are a suspect," Ted replied.

"I will meet you tomorrow at 11:00 p.m., " said the doctor.

"At the spot!"

"No, we must meet in a crowded place. I don't want to get robbed by you."

"Ha! Ha! Ha! " Ted laughed sarcastically. "How about Rich Groceries?"

"That's better. It's the same place where I met you the other day. Right?"

"Right."

When Ted hung up the phone, he went on the Internet to find Mr. Johnson's address. He was successful. After downloading the map to his house, he configured a plan to have him killed for being a party to killing his friend. He thought of a break-in gone badly or a robbery gone badly. He also tried to think of a strategy to get the doctor.

He called his boy Brent, who was a hit man, to discuss plans to finish off Mr. Johnson.

Chapter 29

The Next Day at the Residence

"Mr. Johnson, it's looking pretty good. We should be able to finalize this in the next couple of days. Now, come with me to give Fred the good news," the social worker said cheerfully. "He will be so excited. He has been talking about you and Mrs. Johnson and how he hopes to be with you for life. He's been talking about his strong-looking, new daddy and how he can't wait to get him out on the basketball court. Come on! I love this part of my job. I can't wait to see his face."

The social worker walked down the hall to get Fred while the Johnson's placed their signatures on the documents that would secure their happiness.

As they placed the pen down on the desk, Mr. and Mrs. Johnson heaved a sigh of relief and stood to prepared to see Fred. Everything was just as the social worker said it would be. Fred was very excited about the news of his new family.

Chapter 30

Two for the Price of One

Ted called the hospital. "Hello doc. Did you get in contact with that other guy about the loot?"

"It's looking good. When can you do the job?"

"As soon as you give me half the money." "Well, Ted, I know I said 11:00 p.m. at first, but how about if we push it back to 8:00 p.m.?" "That early?" He raised his voice. "Well, I guess money talks."

"I will see you then," replied the doctor. Later that evening, the doctor received a call for an emergency. He phoned Mr. Johnson. "Hello Mr. Johnson. This is the doctor. I need you to do me another favor."

"Okay, doc. What's up now?"

"I need you to drop off your half of the funds at Rich Groceries."

"In the ghetto?" he said loudly.

"Yeah, the one on King Street near the highway."

"What time? And is it safe?" he asked nervously.

"Yeah. That's why I've got you going when there will still be some daylight and the store will be open."

"What time, man? " Mr. Johnson asked, puffing air in his cheeks.

"Eight o'clock this evening. All right?"

"Now? " he asked with wide eyes.

"Yes, now. I was about to go, but an emergency just came in and I need to tend to it —speaking of which, I need to get back to the floor. You will be there, right?"

"Yeah, I guess."

"Good. Well, he will be parked in the back in a red Buick. All right?"

"All right. This will be the last time — again! Right?"

"Yes."

"It was nice meeting you, " Mr. Johnson said sarcastically.

The doctor hung up the phone and quickly picked it back up to call the drug dealer.

"Hey man! I got Reggie coming in to drop that off."

"Reggie who? Johnson? He's coming all the way from Barry Street?"

"Yeah. How do you know what street he stays on? " the doctor mumbled.

"Oh! " Ted replied, realizing that he wasn't

supposed to know that information. "I told you I know everything. Anyway, does he know where to meet me?"

"You'll be driving your red Buick, right?"

"Yeah, I guess I can."

"Good, because I told him that you would be in that car. He just left, so he should be there shortly. Where are you?"

"I'll be on time. This is business. Bye!"

They hung up.

A small grin crossed Ted's face. "Two for the price of one! " he said to himself.

Then he called Brent, the hit man to tell him the plan.

Chapter 31

Oh, No!

That evening, Ted went to visit Fred at the residential house. Meanwhile, Mr. Johnson was on his way to make the deal.

"I got some good news," Fred announced when he came out of his room and saw Ted waiting for him.

"I got some, too, " Ted responded cheerfully.

"Okay, let me tell you mine first. Remember when I told you that I was going to find out who was responsible for killing your dad. Well, let's just say it's being fixed as we speak."

"Wooo! Thank you, " Fred replied with a wide smile. "You are such a good friend."

"I know," Ted said proudly while Fred gives him a big hug. "Now what's your good news?"

"I found a daddy. I found a daddy," he sang cheerfully.

"Oh, yeah? What's his name?"

"Well, his friends call him R.J. But I call him

Mr. Johnson because my pops and mom said—"
"What's his first name?" Ted cut him off. "It's
... uh ... Reggie."
Oh, no! Ted thought when he realized what he had
just done. "Excuse me for a minute," he said.
Fred looked at him, wondering why his friend
wasn't happy for him.
Ted took the phone out to the hallway to call
Brent, the hit man who was supposed to take care
of Mr. Johnson.
"Hey! Hey! I thought it was you, " the hit man
said. "I guess you are calling to make sure we took
care of business. Well, listen." The man held the
phone up in the air.
"Stop!" Ted screamed.
Bang! Bang! Bang! It was too late. The hit man
put the phone back to his ear. "You see? You can
trust me to handle my business," he said proudly.
"Man, you didn't hear me say stop!"
"What? You didn't want me to kill him? Dude,
you need to make up your mind."
"Man, where are you?"
"We are in an abandoned building on the
riverfront. Oh, yeah! We got some more loot out of
the deal too."
"What do you mean?"
"He got to talking about seeing his new son and
how he would pay anything for us to let him go, so
we had his savings and checking account drained. I
thought to myself how your dead friend John Smith

and how he would never get to see his son again. We let our man believe that we would let him go if he gave us more money. We have decided to share it with you, because we would never have had this job if it wasn't for you."

"Man, you can keep that money and stay the hell out of my face."

"Man! You are just weird! Peace!"

Ted hung up the phone and looked back at Fred's room. He walked the opposite way, because he didn't want to face Fred after having his new dad killed. On the ride home, his phone rang. He looked at the caller ID and the name upset him. It was the doctor.

"Hello. Did you get him? " he asked quickly.

"What?"

"I said, did you get him? Because, I just heard on the hospital scanner that shots were fired at the riverfront. Was that you and the posse taking care of the detective? If so, that's what I am talking about. That was quick. Hey, but you know I am going to need to see the body before I pay you. Right?"

Ted knew he couldn't call the hit man again, because he had just cursed him out. So he called the detective with a plan to set the doctor up.

Chapter 32

The Set-up

"Alright, I will see you tomorrow evening at 6:00, " Ted said into the phone.

"Try to get there a little earlier if you can," suggested the detective, "because my men will be there to set the wiretap. Hey! Don't forget that you must get him to confess to at least one of the crimes in addition to trying to have me killed."

The next day at 6:00 p.m. sharp, the wiretap was set up.

"How are you going to breathe in a garbage bag in the trunk?" Ted asked the detective while the police officer tapes a small mike to his chest.

"Look at this!" He showed Ted some tubes. "These are oxygen tubes that will allow me to breathe for at least four hours in a tight place."

"Then, how are you going to hear us?"

"Do you mind wearing a wire?"

"Normally, I would, but this man has to go. Otherwise, I might be the next one to come into his emergency room, and he might let me die or kill me because of the dirt I have on him, " Ted said.

"Come on! Let's get into the van so we can get you hooked up, " said Detective Mac. "Plus I have to put on my make-up to make me look dead."

When the officers finished preparing Ted's wire, they parked their unmarked car in the parking lot and tried to look like regular customers. Ted and the detective walked behind the car and opened the trunk of Ted's car.

"I thought I told you to clean out your trunk," the detective said.

"My bad! Dead man walking," Ted mumbled with a grin.

"Man! Just move that stuff," the detective responded playfully.

"You don't have broken needles in here, do you?"

"No! What would I have that for? I never use my own supply."

"Alright!"

The detective lay down in the trunk and positioned himself to be as comfortable as possible.

"Your backseat armrest —leave that down, and I will try to listen through that spot."

"Alright. Can I close this now? The time is getting close," Ted said with both hands on the top of the trunk.

"Yeah, you'd better. This could be the one time a doctor is early for something. I will call you in a minute so we can communicate and so you can warn me of the doctor's arrival."

"Alright."

The detective called Ted in the driver's seat. They made small talk about the sting and how Ted was thinking of starting a family.

"Can you hear me? " asked the detective.

"Yes. Can you hear me?"

"Yes, I can hear you now, " Ted responded thinking of the commercial.

"This is off the record, but what do you think about me getting a son?"

"Are you about to have a baby?"

"No. I mean adopting a child."

"What? You're thinking of adopting? Man, I'd better start going to church. People always speaks about how God can change people. Are you in church now?"

"No! I just promised my friend something."

"Was it a promise or a bet?"

"A promise, smart ass! But you know what, it was more like an agreement."

"So, what happened, why are you selling? Look at how you turned out! " the detective replied sarcastically.

"This was my choice. Now that I see what this path leads to, I want to stop. But selling drugs is almost like using them. You can get addicted."

"Hey! Isn't your wire on?"

"Yeah, I think so, " Ted replied looking down in his shirt.

"You know you just said that you sell drugs!"

"Oops!"

"Don't worry. When we pull this off, I will take care of it."

"Good, because —! Uh oh! " he stopped the flow of the conversation. "I think I see him, " Ted said with excitement.

"Okay. I am in position. Make sure you leave the phone on. That way, I can hear, too."

"Okay, I gotta go." Ted said quickly as he closed the flap on the phone. The next moment, he realized that the detective had just asked him to not hang up the phone so he could hear the conversation with the doctor. He didn't try to call him back, because the doctor had pulled up right beside his car, and Ted didn't want him to get suspicious. The drug dealer waved the doctor to come in and sit down.

"Hey!"

"Why are you looking all down?" said Dr. Cashion.

"Because I was thinking about what you told me about the guy you had killed so you could give his heart to that little boy."

"Man! Anyway ..."

"I am just wondering how you did such a thing."

The doctor narrowed his eyes, paused, and said, "You aren't wearing a wire are you? " He abruptly thrust his hand out to check Ted's body. Luckily,

Ted was able to push his hand back just before he felt something.

"What do you take me for? A snitch?"

"Well, anyway, this is a totally different issue. Where is the body?"

"It's in the trunk."

"Well, come on! Let's see it."

The drug dealer and the doctor exited the car and walked to the rear of the vehicle. As they walked, the doctor asked, "Hey! You aren't getting weak on me, are you?"

"Man, no! " he responded. "I got it, " he said as he positioned the keys to open the trunk.

"Hey! I really appreciate you doing this."

"Yeah! It's not every day I kill someone," said Ted.

"Yeah, right! People like you are the reason a lot of us doctors work so hard."

Ted opened the trunk, and inside he saw a black bag.

"Can I see him?" asked the doctor.

"Sure."

Ted pulled down the top portion of the bag and inside they saw a pale-faced detective.

"Yep! I know what death looks like," the doctor said as he laid the cover back over his face.

"You should!" Ted said with a little smirk.

"Anyway, here you go! Thank you."

The detective had had enough. He burst open the bag and grabbed the doctor. At the same time, a swarm of police cars pulled up along with a van.

"Read him his rights," the detective ordered one of the officers.

"No! No! No! " Ted screamed. "I thought you were going to arrest him at the hospital. Now, everybody is going to think I work with cops!"

The detective pulled him to the side.

"He wasn't giving you concrete statements. Now at least we can say he was at the scene and maybe a jury will find that enough to convict him."

They put the doctor into the squad car, and the doctor just stared at the dealer. When the dealer caught his eyes, the doctor moved his mouth expressing, I am going to kill you.

"Can I go? " Ted asked the detective sadly.

"I am going to need you to give a statement," the detective said, holding a pad in front of him.

"Hey! I told you over and over that I don't want to be known as a snitch," Ted responded as he pushed the pad away.

"How about writing a statement and remaining anonymous?"

"Okay. You know, after this, I am out of this game for good."

"Good! Tell me, did anything happen here that brought that about?"

"No. Do you remember that earlier I was talking about adoption? Well, I may have a little boy looking up to me."

"Oh, all right, then. I will be in touch. And don't forget that statement."

"Don't worry! I know the sooner I do it, the sooner I will be done with you."

Chapter 33

Mr. Johnson Is Missing

"Hello, Phil? Have you heard from or seen my husband." asked Mrs. Johnson.

"No, I haven't. Why do you ask?"

"Well, I haven't seen him or heard from him in almost a day."

"Have you called the police?"

"I will call them when I get off the phone with you."

"Okay. Well, if I hear from him, I will have him call you. Don't worry! He will be home soon." She hung up the phone and dialed 911.

The operator answered. "911. Is this an emergency?"

"Yes this is. My husband is missing," said Mrs. Johnson.

"How long has he been gone?"

"For a day."

"Okay, I'll have a police officer over there soon."

The police officer arrived.

"Mrs. Johnson, when was the last time you seen him, " asked the officer.

"Yesterday. He told me that he had something to do for our doctor."

"Does this doctor have a name?"

"Dr. Cashion."

"Is that right?" he said curiously.

"Yeah, that's right. Do you know him?"

"Well, he was just arrested out there in the hood. I think he was trying to hire a hit man to kill a detective."

"Oh, no! This has gone too far."

"What did you say? What has gone too far?" the officer inquired.

"Nothing," she said. Then she closed her eyes and sighed.

"Look, I think I have enough information. I will call you if I need anymore details."

The officer returned to the precinct and passed the information to the detective. When the detective found out that the missing person was associated with Dr. Cashion, he immediately went to question the doctor.

"Doctor Cashion, do you know a Reggie Johnson?"

"Yes, I remember him. I tried to save his son."

"Okay, that's another case," he mumbled sarcastically. "But anyway, when was the last time you saw him?"

"I haven't seen him or heard from him since his

son died. By the way, " he paused, "I am saying nothing more until my lawyer is here."

"Okay. Thanks for your help," the detective replied without becoming defensive.

The detective knew the doctor wasn't telling him everything, because he had received a copy of Mr.

Johnson's phone records before he went to speak to him. They showed that Dr. Cashion had called Mr. Johnson several times before he came up missing.

He lied! Now the question is why, he thought. He was suspicious that the doctor was involved in Mr. Johnson's disappearance.

The detective wanted to build a stronger case in the wrongful death of a patient, but he felt the case that he had hired a hit man to kill an officer was stronger because of the evidence from the set-up.

Chapter 34

Court

"All rise!" announced the bailiff. The judge was about to enter the courtroom. When he was seated in his big black chair, the bailiff gestured that the audience should sit down.

"This is the case of Dr. Bill Cashion vs. the State in the attempted murder of a police officer. Prosecutor, state your case," announced the judge.

"Your Honor, this is the case of a doctor gone bad in an attempt to hide evidence from the wrongful death of a patient."

"Objection! This is not what this case is about" said the doctor's attorney.

"Sustained! Stick to the case, will you!"

"Yes, Your Honor," she responded with a sigh. "Anyway, during this case you will find evidence of the doctor making deals with an informer, who would like to remain unknown to protect his safety. However, we will forward a written statement signed by the informer regarding the doctor's agreement with him. We will also furnish information from a sting that was set up to prove the doctor's involvement in the conspiracy to kill the detective."

"Objection, Your Honor! He wasn't convicted during that time."

"Overruled! He was a suspect," replied the judge staring at the defendant's lawyer.

"Well, Your Honor, we would like to let things stand here for now and prove our case."

"Defendant!" announced the judge.

"Jury, please forgive the State Attorney's rudeness in not acknowledging your presence. Good afternoon, Judge and Ladies and Gentlemen of the Jury. Court, this is a case of picking on a good doctor. He has saved the lives of many teenagers who have been brought to his emergency room and needed operations."

The prosecutor cut in. "Objection! Your honor, the court didn't ask for a character statement."

"Your Honor, I am just trying to give the jury a better outlook on what kind of doctor he is. This is not meant to justify the case. It's background information."

"Overruled! But make it brief," said the judge to the doctor's attorney.

"Thank you, Your Honor." The defense attorney rolled her eyes at the prosecutor. He looked back at the jury. "This doctor won several awards for his participation in the invention of instruments to help keep people alive. He's also won several community awards, such as the Most Valuable List and Role Model Award. He captured the attention of many interns who are grateful to be able to work under him."

"Our doctor hopes that the people would never think of him as a violent person. He is in the business of saving lives — not destroying them. In the course of my proof, I will present his co-workers and you will see how they respect the doctor. You will also see how his character does not match the character of a man who would commit the act that he is accused of. " The attorney stopped and stared at the jury in silence.

"Anything else?" the judge asked.

"No, Your Honor. The defense rests."

"Okay. Call your first witness."

"Your Honor, I would like to call Detective MacIntosh, the officer on this case."

As the detective walked to the bench, the prosecutor stood to approach the bench. The doctor's attorney flipped through his pages to find the questions he had prepared for this witness.

"Please state your name and who you are for the records," said the prosecutor.

"My name is Leonard McIntosh, detective for the Barry County Police Department."

"Thank you, detective. Please state when you first met the doctor and how he acted."

"I first met him at St. Mill's hospital in his

office and that day he acted very strange, as if he was trying to hide something."

"Objection! Speculation!"

"Your Honor, this man is a detective. Don't you think he would know if someone was acting suspicious or not? If not, I think this would be an insult to his profession."

"I see your point. Overruled!" said the judge.

"Detective, what did the doctor say or do?"

"Well, there was a lot of information he volunteered that he probably should not know unless he was right there at the scene. And, oh yeah on his desk, he had the folder of a worker who had just died suspiciously at the hospital."

"Who was she?"

"Her name was Patricia Dorsey."

"How did she die?"

"Objection! Your honor, what does this have to do with this case?"

"Your Honor, I am trying to show the jury that this doctor had a motive to kill the detective," replied the prosecutor.

"Overruled! Proceed."

"Well, she was said to have had an overdose on drugs, but witnesses say that they know for a fact that she hadn't used drugs since she became pregnant. Ms. Dorsey was later found in the file room down in the hospital basement.

"Do you think the doctor killed her?" "Objection! Your honor, he is trying to make this another case."

"Again, Your Honor, I will show the court how this all comes together."

"Overruled! Proceed!"

"It is my knowledge that Ms. Dorsey was in a relationship with a man who died in the hospital two days earlier."

"Who are we speaking of? " asked the prosecutor.

"The guy who was on the news as John Doe, but whose real name they found out later — John Smith. Ms. Dorsey, who was his long term girlfriend and the mother of his child, worked at the hospital where he ended up dying. The coroner said he couldn't complete the diagnosis because his heart was missing. His heart was missing because supposedly a rich man's son needed a heart, and John Smith's heart was allegedly taken for the boy. Anyway, that's another case. Ms. Dorsey found John Smith's wallet and his ID said that he was not a donor. Assuming that she brought this information to the doctor's attention—"

The doctor's lawyer cuts in. "Objection! Speculation!"

"Sustained."

"Well, I know that she brought it to his attention, because of her co-workers statements." the detective continued. "Dr. Cashion had a motive to get rid of that evidence. So, me being an intrigue detective ... decided to get a warrant to investigate the doctor's office when he wasn't present. I found Ms. Dorsey's file on Dr. Cashion's desk, and it stated that she had been in drug rehab years earlier. I put two and two together and presumed— "

The other lawyer cut in again and slammed down his note pad. "Your Honor, speculation again!"

"Your Honor, this is a detective speaking," replied the prosecutor.

"I agree. Overruled! But this is sounding like a case for Pat Dorsey, so get to the reason we are here."

"Yes, Your Honor."

"Go ahead, Detective. What did you presume?" asked the prosecutor.

"I presumed that the doctor found out that she had been on drugs and decided to give her a drug overdose. A statement by an informer said this is what he did."

"You have a statement!" The defense attorney intervenes. "Who is this informer? I heard he was a drug dealer. His testimony bears no weight. He isn't a trusted citizen in society."

"Attorney, please be advised that you will get a turn to cross examine the witness. If you have another outburst, we will have a big problem. There will be order in this courtroom!" stated the judge.

"Forgive me, Your Honor," the lawyer said, looking down and taking his seat.

"As I said," the detective continued, "I have a signed statement.

"I have no further questions for this witness, Your Honor," said the prosecutor.

"Defendant, proceed," said the judge.

"Jurors, allow me to apologize for the prosecutor wasting your time on something that doesn't pertain to this case. Now, Detective —. Can I call you detective?"

"Yes, that's what I am."

"How long have you been a detective?"

"About three years."

"Three years, and you have come with all these assumptions! Detective, what I would like to know is how do you know your informer, or the person who wrote that statement? I mean, isn't he a drug dealer?"

"Well, I don't really know at this point, but there are some speculations. This is because I think your client is his best customer."

The prosecutor smirked.

"Please, Detective, this point is about your character. I mean, how can you pick such a poor character to act as your informer?"

"Well, I never said that he was a drug dealer. He has never been convicted."

"Yes! But if we leave it up to you, he'll never be convicted," the doctor's lawyer said, giving him a deep stare.

"Was that a question?" asked the detective,

looking brave and self-assured.

"No, but this is. How do you know the informer, the drug dealer?"

"Objection! Your Honor, the plaintiff is trying to badger my witness."

"Sustained. Just call the person the Informer, since he doesn't want to be recognized by name."

The doctor's attorney and the judge looked at the detective and waited for his response.

"What was your question?" the detective asked to give him more time to think of a good answer.

"How do you know your informer, the drug dealer?"

"Objection! Your Honor, defendant is trying to desensitize the jurors by calling his contact names."

"Sustained! Just call the person the Informer, since he doesn't want to be recognized by name," the judge said, giving the doctor's attorney a hard stare.

"Well, again, how do you know the Informer?"

"I met him through a mutual friend."

"Does this friend have a name?"

"I forgot his last name, but his first name is Tommy."

"Okay, I see we are not going to get anywhere with this," responded the defendant's lawyer as he walked back to his desk and flipped the pages that lay there.

The prosecutor raises her pencil, and gives him

an intense stare, and when he notice her, she moves her mouth to say thank you.

"Now, I have two more questions," said the defense attorney. "The first one is, why did he decide to be your informer?"

"Well, he wants to be a cop."

"Is that why, or did you promise never to arrest him for drug trafficking. Come on! Tell the jury something believable."

"Objection, Your Honor! Badgering the witness."

"Sustained," said the judge. There was a brief silence. "Are there any further questions?" asked the judge breaking the silence.

"Yes, Your Honor. I said I have two questions." He turned back to the detective. "You said earlier that you think my client was the informer's favorite customer. Are you admitting that he was selling drugs?"

"Are you admitting that the doctor was doing drugs?"

"Detective, I am the one doing the questioning. I have no further questions, Your Honor."

"Does the prosecutor care to redirect?"

"No, Your Honor. The prosecution rests."

"Do you mind if we close the first day a little early and resume tomorrow at nine o'clock?"

"No, Your Honor. I don't mind."

"Do you mind, prosecutor?" asked the judge. "No, I don't mind," she said, moving her head from left to right.

"In that case, we will proceed tomorrow morning at nine o'clock."

The doctor returned to his private cell. It had been a long day, and he lay on his bed, wondering how he had got himself in this position. He starts thinking about that day when Mr. Smith was rushed into the hospital. He thinks about that day until he falls asleep for the next day in court.

Chapter 35

Night Stick

Court is in session and Dr. Cashion is sitting on the bench. He noticed an attorney turned facing the jury. The attorney appears to be on the prosecutor's team. The attorney is telling the juror some remarks about the case.

"Ladies and gentleman of the jury, allow me to give my remarks of that day. He sighs and pauses. A man was rushed into the hospital unconscious. The only thought in his head was getting back to his son to take him to McDonald's and a movie. Anyway to make a long story short, during his time of unconsciousness this man had an out of body experience. This was during the time his heart was being taken out without his permission. At the same time of his and I quote, 'murder surgery,' he hears his girlfriend Patricia Dorsey on the floor and he suddenly remembered her telling him about the emergency training she took. So, he turns the heart monitor back on after Dr. Cashion had turned it off so he can get her attention."

Dr. Cashion begins wondering how the attorney knows all that. He stares harder at him and then he realized the attorney has on a filthy suit.

"When she tried to come into the room, a nurse stopped her because if Pat would have came in the room and saw him lying there with no heart; all hell was going to break loose. Tell me what gave the doctor the right to take this man's heart like that?" The attorney asked the juror taking a second to look at them.

At this time Dr. Cashion stood up in disbelief continuing to wonder how the attorney knows all this. He noticed a mop inside a bucket by the corner wall.

"So when Pat was going down on the elevator, he had his spirit to move inside her. But she ignored his attempts. Again later, Mr. Smith had his spirit to move in her again. He wanted her to pay more attention to the news anchor talking about him. She did pay attention this time especially when the anchor mentioned the movie and McDonald's coupons. Anyway, eventually she found out that man in the hospital was her man and that he wasn't a donor." He said walking towards the mop inside the bucket. "She was going to make it her business to get to the bottom of his distorted crime. But the doctor murdered her."

"Ladies and Gentlemen of the Jury I guess by now the question you may be asking yourself is: how do I know all of this? He said as he wrings out the mop. "I will tell you how I know all this."

Dr. Cashion leans forward to see and hear the man better.

The man turns around slowly. "Because I am that man, Mr. Smith Pat's boyfriend." he said looking Dr. Cashion directly in his eyes. "We had a son. " Mr. Smith added pointing the stick at him and taking quick steps towards him.

Dr. Cashion swiftly stood up being frighten out of his sleep. "What the... ! " He said fighting a guard's night stick away from his body.

"Are you alright?" asked the guard when he noticed Dr. Cashion frightening expression.

"Yes, I just had a weird dream. Why are you poking me with that night stick?" he asked as he sat up in the bed.

"Oh. I was trying to get your attention to ask you what time you need to be woke for court tomorrow?" asked the guard putting the night stick back on his belt.

"Eight o'clock. Courts at nine o'clock." Dr. Cashion answered as he lay back down and started to think about how his bad habits got him in this predicament.

He moved around to position himself and get more comfortable. When he became still he started thinking about the party after his graduation and the first time he used drugs.

Knock! Knock! Knock! "Hey Doc! Are you ready?"

As the young doctor answered the door, he took in the fact that he was being called a doctor for the first time.

"Hello doctor. What's up? " said Kelvin and Brian, his classmates.

"The graduation party is what's up."

"Let's get a little high before we dash over there," Kelvin said.

Then Kelvin pulled out a bag of drugs. "Say, it's about time you brought something to the table," Brian said in a sarcastic manner.

"Hey man! I am a doctor now and I will be bringing a lot to the table."

They all gave each other high-fives.

"Hey doctor! Fix us a drink since you don't get high," said Kelvin.

"This is not my house."

"I am not talking about you. I mean the other doctor!"

"He knew that," said Cashion. "He was just being silly! Make sure you don't waste those drugs on the floor," he continued.

"What, you still aren't doing drugs yet? I heard a lot of doctors are doing this to relieve themselves from the pressures. You may as well get started now."

"No thanks. I think I am cool."

"You think? Okay! He is getting weak."

Everyone started to laugh. Minutes went by as they laughed and talked about old times at school.

"Do you guys remember when this guy was going to fail a class because he hadn't operated on his corpse correctly?" said Cashion.

"Yeah, I remember him. Whatever happened to him, anyway?" responded Kelvin.

"Oh, I heard he decided to drop out because he didn't think himself fit to be a doctor after that," said Brian.

"What about him, though?" Brian glanced at Dr. Cashion.

"Now, what you do?" Kelvin asked as he turned his head to look at Cashion.

"I am so sorry, but I took his corpse's parts because I didn't cut mines right. I cut all my pieces wrong. I was either going to get a fail or steal somebody else's parts. I guess you know what I chose."

"That's messed up, doctor, but I understand." Dr. Cashion smirked. "As a matter of fact, I think I saw him drugged out the other day."

"That's sad, " said Kelvin and Brian.

"Man, I did whatever I had to do to become a doctor. I wasn't interested in not graduating. I did what I had to do," Cashion replied with a slight smile.

They continued to talk and joke, and soon it was getting close to party time.

"Are we ready to go? " asked Kelvin.

"Yeah. Let's go have some groovy fun, " said Dr. Cashion.

"Did he just say groovy?" Kelvin asked with a half smile.

"I guess you are high," said Brian, smirking.

"Let's go, " said Kelvin.

"Go ahead of me, " said Dr. Cashion. "I will be there in a minute."

The visitors walked towards the door, and the doctor straightened up the mess. He realized that they had left some drugs on the table. While staring at them for a minute, he thought about taking them. *I wonder what the hype is behind this stuff,* he thought.

Onk, onk, onk, the car horn blew, notifying him that his friends were in a hurry and ready to go. "O, yeah! Right!"

The doctor picked up his keys and ran out the door. The group arrived at the house where the party was being held, and everybody appeared to be drunk or high. Kelvin pushed the button for the door bell.

Ring! Ring! Ring!

"Someone's ringing the doorbell?" one of the guests called out. "You know the door is already opened. He doesn't have a doorman yet."

The newcomers walked in, and everyone giggled and hugged each other the way old drinking buddies do. The host escorted everyone down to the basement.

"Hey! Watch your step. We are not stopping our party for your injuries, although we all could use the practice," said the host with a smile.

As Dr. Cashion and his friends entered the basement, the sounds of some old school music were in the mix. When the others saw them, they let out a big roar. One of them held up a hose attached to a cage to inform them that there was free beer. Another guy displayed little packets of cocaine that he was willing to share with anyone. The new arrivals went their separate ways. Dr. Cashion noticed a friend sitting in the corner drinking what looked like beer.

"Hey man! What you got there?" said Cashion.

"Hey, what's up? How are you? " asked George, one of Cashion's study buddies.

"I was fine until I smelled your breath."

They both laughed. While they were laughing, one of the guys came over handed Cashion a mug of beer.

"Here, man. I got this for you. Who is your friend?" he said.

"Oh, everybody has the same name —Doctor," George said, extending his hand to shake the stranger's hand.

"Hey, I am Dr. Cashion."

"Oh, yeah! Cash, huh? Because you will make a lot of cash."

They all giggled.

"Now that we got acquainted, what's up with this party?" the friend asked.

"It's cool, but a lot of people are still packing. A lot of people are taking vacations before going to residence. As a matter of fact, are you supposed to be leaving tomorrow?" asked George.

"Yeah, the keyword is supposed," said Cashion. They all laughed until someone asked another question.

"Hey, didn't we have a class together?" asked another party-goer.

"I don't know. Uh ... did you take immunology last semester?"

"No, I took that two years ago. " responded the approaching person?

During the conversation, Cashion noticed someone in the room doing drugs. The man looked up and noticed Cashion watching him. He smiled with powder all over his mustache. *What do they see in that stuff?* Cashion wondered.

That night, everyone had so much fun. They laughed at anything — someone looking stupid or just being silly. Sometimes they laughed to break any silence. Some ladies did come by, and some of the guys got lucky. Everybody ended up with someone he had been checking out all year. A young lady who Cashion had met on the first day of school came in and recognized him.

"Hey you! How come you never called me?" she said with her arms crossed.

"Well, we didn't major in the same subject, so I didn't have time to call you."

"Whatever. You got some coke?"

"At home," said Cashion, joking.

"Oh! Let's go to your house then."

"I came with my friends."

"So did I, but I think they all have other rides now."

"Well, let me tell my friends, and you do the same."

They arrived at Cashion's place. It was lucky for him that he had taken an extra bag from his friend, who was lying on the couch at the party.

They indulged in some conversation while she indulged in the drug and smoked some weed she had in her purse. She took a puff and extended her hand so Cashion could take a hit.

"Why not?" he responded.

Moments later, the lady asked, "Tell me, doctor. What are you going to do when the first person dies on you?"

"I am going to have a party."

They laughed.

"Why did you say that?"

"Because who knows? We could be doing that person a favor by letting him die. Death might be the best thing for him, if he is poor and has no insurance."

"Hey! Did you remember your oath?"

"Yeah. That's all I did —I memorized it. You

know the real world is much deeper than that." "You think?" she responded and took another snort.

"Man, what do you guys get from letting that powder up your nose?"

"There's only one way to find out. I dare you!"

I am easy when it comes to dares, he thought.

Cashion bent over the desk and started sniffing.

The rush he got was unheard of. The next day, he didn't remember a thing that had happened that night. All he remembered was the rush he got when he took the first sniff. He has been hooked ever since.

In the morning, the sound of the guard's night stick clattering the bars on the doctor's cell woke him up. "Are you ready for court?" asked the guard.

"I will be ready in a minute," the doctor responded as he put on his pants.

Chapter 36

The Next Day in Court

The bailiff had the audience stand before the judge arrived and sit down after he was seated.

"Ladies and gentlemen of the court, this is the second day of the proceedings of Dr. Cashion versus the State. I think we left off with the defendant," said the judge.

"Yes, Your Honor. That's correct," said the defense attorney. "Good morning, Judge, ladies and gentlemen of the jury, prosecutor, and witnesses."

Everybody nodded their head in greeting.

The attorney continued. "Court, I believe I left off providing evidence that this detective shows very bad character when picking his friends. I told you that his so-called informer is a popular drug dealer. That may be the reason why he would rather be anonymous than give his name."

"Objection! Speculation!"

"Sustained! Next question."

"Your Honor. I have nothing further."

"Prosecutor, call your next witness."

"Your Honor, I would like to call the receptionist at the hospital, Janice Webb."

Janice walked in looking remorseful.

Please state your name for the court."

"Janice Webb."

"Ms. Webb, how long have you known Dr. Cashion?"

"I guess for about five years."

"How did you come to know him? " She counted on her fingers. "One, two ... uh ... three ... yeah! It is four-and-a-half years, to be exact. Well, I came to know him when I first started working."

"In your opinion, what kind of doctor is he?"

"I don't know. Some days he is calm and other days he is hyper."

"What do you mean?"

"He's just moving." She used her two index fingers to make the motion of someone walking fast. "He hardly ever stays still."

"Ms. Webb, have you seen anyone on drugs?"

"Yeah," she said, thinking, *Who hasn't?*

"Can you tell if the doctor was on drugs?"

"Objection! Witness is not sitting at the bench to imply that the doctor uses drugs."

"Your Honor, the witness was a former drug user herself and stayed in a home with other drug users. She should have some experience with detecting when someone is on drugs."

"Prosecutor, I am not interested in becoming a laughingstock. Sustained! Next question."

"Yes, Your Honor. Ms. Webb, do you remember Patricia Dorsey?"

"Yes, poor lady! I was her rehab partner. She was supposed to tell me if she was having a relapse."

The doctor's attorney looked restless and sighs.

The judge stares at him with evil eyes.

"From your knowledge, did she show signs of being back on drugs?"

"Your Honor, objection!" said the defense attorney. "First of all, again, she is not in the capacity of a professional in this case. Second, the death of Ms. Patricia Dorsey is not what we are holding this trial for."

"Your Honor, how many times must we go over this? I am trying to show motive."

"The court will stand at recess while the two lawyers will meet me in my chambers," ordered the judge.

"I want to ask the detective to join us, " the prosecutor said as she stared at the defendant's lawyer.

"Do you object?" the judge asked the defendant's lawyer.

"I guess it wouldn't hurt. It's not as though he is on trial." The attorney looked at his client and winked to assure him that it was all right.

"In that case, the court is at recess for fifteen minutes," said the judge.

The lawyers exited towards the judge's chamber while the bailiff walked to the defendant to see if he needed to go to the restroom. Then he turned to the jury and instructed them to not discuss the case until court was over.

"Have a seat," the judge said as he took off his robe. He looked at the detective. "Now, why is he in here?"

"Your Honor, he was in the process of discovering all the evidence before he put on his sting."

"Well, in this court we brought up two deaths. John Smith and a Patricia Dorsey. I haven't heard any evidence for the attempted murder of the detective."

"Your Honor, I am leading up to that."

The doctor's lawyer cut her off. "We know! We know you are trying to show motive."

The prosecutor rolled her eyes.

"Tell me, he continued, are you planning on bringing up the man who has been missing? His son got John Smith's heart, right? Please don't say that the doctor had something to do with that. Like everything else, it was just a coincidence."

"That's right. You are wasting the court's time," said the judge. "Can we get to the meat of this case? This case is not about whether Cashion had motive or not, but whether he was attempting to kill you. " The judge pointed at the detective.

"Yes, Your Honor. I see your point."

"How about if I give you another day to arrange to get to the meat of this case and close court for today."

Both lawyers moved their head up and down in agreement.

The crowd had come back into the court room after the fifteen-minute break.

The judge entered the room and said, "The court is going to make this a very short day. We will close for now and resume tomorrow at 9:00 a.m."

The judge stood up and asked the bailiff to dismiss the crowd.

Chapter 37

Can You Still Adopt Me?

Several months had passed, And there was still no sign of Mr. Johnson. Mrs. Johnson started thinking about the kid at the home and wondered if he was getting worried. She went to visit him.

"Hi Fred," Mrs. Johnson said when she saw him eating a chocolate bar.

Fred stood up and gave her the strongest hug. She sighed, because she really needed that hug.

"I was so worried about you, " said Fred. "Are you all right? Has Mr. Johnson came back yet?"

"I am afraid not, " she replied sadly.

"Can you still adopt me?" He gave her another strong hug. Mrs. Johnson looked in his eyes and couldn't stand to lose him too.

"If the paperwork is still underway and if everything checks out okay, then sure."

"Thank you! Thank you! And thank you! " He gave her a third hug.

To get things off Mrs. Johnson's mind, they played games together. At the end of the afternoon, Mrs. Johnson left the adoption home smiling, but when she arrived at home, she was sad again and worried about her hubby. The following day, the drug dealer, Ted, visited the child.

"Hey! Can I see Fred?" asked the drug dealer.

"You know," said Phil the social worker, "you ran out of here so fast during your last visit. I saw you on the phone; did you get some bad news or something?"

"Well, yes. Anyway, can I see him?"

"Well he got some bad news too. He found out that his possible new dad has been missing for almost a month. This is a lot for a child to take."

"Yeah, I know. How is he taking this?"

"Well, he just got a visit from Mrs. Johnson," said Phil. "That helped. I think she is still going to go through with the adoption."

"For real!" Ted said, excited for the child.

"Yep. Isn't it amazing that she's thinking of taking him, though she knows that he may not have a father?"

"Well, I would like to act as a father figure for him. Do you think she would mind if I come by sometimes?"

"I am sure she won't mind the help. Wait a minute. How are we going to count Mr. Johnson out? He still may come back."

Ted puts his head down.

"Can I see Fred?" he asked softly.

"Sure. Come on, " the social worker said, and he took a step towards Fred's room.

When Ted and Tom entered the room, the boy gave Ted a hug.

"Guess what! I got two bits of good news today. First, Mrs. Johnson might still adopt me. Second, you took care of my father's mur— "

Before he could finish his sentence, the drug dealer screamed "Car!" and put his hand over the child's mouth.

"Yeah, Mercury! Yeah, Mercury!" he repeated. "But you can't tell anybody yet, because I wanted to surprise everyone."

Fred looked at Ted and saw that he was serious about telling this lie, so he went along with him.

"Yeah, the Mercury," he replied shamefully.

"Yeah, I told you to keep this a secret. Can you excuse us for a minute?" Ted said, turning towards the social worker.

"Sure! I didn't hear anything about a car, " the social worker whispered with a slight smile and walked out the door.

"Hey man! Do you know how many people you will hurt if you tell anybody that I took care of the guy who was responsible for killing your daddy? You may even hurt Mrs. Johnson, and I know that she doesn't want to be hurt anymore. So make sure you keep that a secret. Come on! Let's shake on it like men. Because you are giving me your word that you will keep this a secret."

The drug dealer gave Fred a firm handshake, and the child tried to give him one back.

"Now, don't break your word, because you won't be a man, and I only come by to see men. That's why I am here today. By the way, speaking of Mrs. Johnson, do you think she would mind if I come by to see you sometimes?"

"I am sure she won't mind. You are good for me. You help me remember what kind of man my father was. Some of the kids in here have never seen or heard from their daddy. But Mrs. Johnson is so sweet and pretty, and I am sure she wouldn't mind."

"Good, because I am moving up here soon, and I will need someone to go to McDonald's and a movie with me."

The child started crying.

"What's wrong?" asked Ted.

"My dad was going to take me to McDonald's and a movie the day he died."

"Oh! My bad!"

They continued to talk on throughout the day. Before Ted left, he was stopped by the social worker.

"Hey Ted! I decided to have you meet Mrs. Johnson before he leaves this place. How about if I set something up in a couple of weeks?"

"Good! Fred and I are supposed to go to a movie in a couple of weeks. Maybe she can go with us."

"I will let her know and see what she says."

"I hope everything goes well, because I have to fix this."

"Oh no! Are you a fix-it person, too? Because Mr. Johnson was a fix-it type of person. Hey! If you want to try to get on Mrs. Johnson's good side, please don't show that side of yourself."

"Thanks for the advice," said Ted, because he wanted to make a good impression.

Chapter 38

Back in Court

The prosecutor asked to approach the bench, and the judge agreed. Everybody in the room looked at each other, wondering what was going on this time. The attorneys finished talking and took their seats. Seconds later, the judge spoke.

"Ladies and Gentlemen of the court," said the judge with a smirk, "believe it or not, you may be hearing closing arguments today. Let's see what happens. Prosecutor, call your first witness."

"Your Honor, I would like to call a surprise witness: Mr. Ted Humphrey."

The judge looked at the doctor's attorney. "Do you have a problem with this?" he asked.

"No, he is not a surprise," he replied with a smile.

"Proceed."

Ted, the drug dealer, walked up wearing a plaid suit, a matching silk tie, and, of course, alligator shoes.

"Please state your name for the court," the

prosecutor said as she fumbled through her papers.

"Ted Humphrey."

"Can you please tell us how you and the defendant know each other?"

"I sold him drugs," he replied, looking at the doctor. The doctor avoided eye contact.

"When did you sell him drugs?"

"The same day that Pat Dorsey was reported missing."

"Do you know Ms. Dorsey?"

"Yes, I know her very well. She was my partner's girlfriend."

"Who? The one who died without a heart?"

"Yeah. You know, I heard that he wasn't even a donor."

"You heard right. But it was true because his license stated that he was not a donor."

"Your Honor!" the defendant's attorney yelled noticing that that question has nothing to do with this case.

The prosecutor smiled and chuckled.

"So, why are you here helping out your friend like this?"

"Because, I gave him my word."

"And what was that?"

"Well, believe it or not, back in my school days I used to get picked on a lot. He used to take up for me. I think it's about time I did something for him. I am here for him, and nobody else."

"You sound like a very good friend." She sighed. "Now, you said earlier that you sold a drug to the doctor on the same day that Patricia Dorsey died."

"Yes."

"Did you ever hear from him again?"

"Yes. I heard from him one day."

"What did he ask for?"

"He said that he was in trouble and that he needed to get out."

"What did he need?"

"He confessed to taking John's heart without his permission or the permission of a family member. He felt that the detective was getting close to finding out that he killed John and took his heart."

The doctor's lawyer cut in. "Objection! Speculation!"

"Sustained. Please don't assume anything when being examined," instructed the judge.

"Yes, judge," Ted said as he turned and made eye contact with the judge. "Anyway, little did he know that John was a good friend of mine. So, I just let him go on and on about what he had done."

"What about the detective? I guess Dr. Cashion didn't know you two were acquainted?"

"No, he didn't," Ted responded, and he glanced at the detective.

"Tell me what happened that day on the sting."

Ted described what had happened on the sting.

He gave precise details, as if he had been the detective. The detective looked impressed, because he knew that Ted would have made a good cop; he appeared to know all the terminology.

"Anyway," Ted continued, "Cashion asked to see the body. When we went back to the trunk, he thought he was looking at a dead man. I believe that since he had no idea that he was being set up, he didn't bother to check the detective's pulse."

"So he saw the body and gave you the money. Right?"

"Objection! Leading the witness."

"Sustained."

"Ted Humphrey, did you accept any money for the killing of the detective?"

"Yes."

"No further questions, Your Honor. The prosecution rests."

"Your witness," said the judge as he checked his watch.

"Thank you, Your Honor. Mr. Humphrey, earlier in your testimony, you mentioned that you gave the doctor a drug."

Ted shook his head in agreement.

"Please speak out loud," the defense attorney said.

"Yes, " said Ted.

"Are you saying that the doctor trusted you to commit a murder for him because you gave him one drug?"

Ted looked confused.

"I know that this may not look good for the doctor. I know that you and the doctor had a seller-customer relationship or a friendship. Whatever it was, you and the doctor had built a relationship. So, basically, you sold drugs to the doctor, and now you are using the court as some kind of get-back to the doctor. What was the real reason for doing this? Because you were afraid that the doctor would turn you in?"

"Man, whatever!"

"Hmmm, whatever, huh? You see, jury, what we are really dealing with is a drug dealer trying to get the doctor for something. I guess that he really believed that the doctor had killed his friend and/or that the detective is trying to get the doctor convicted to make himself look good, especially since this is a high profile case."

The detective smirked slightly and put his head down.

"Yes, he did kill my friend!" Ted shouted, getting upset.

"Did he kill him, or was he already dead? Since this keeps coming up, here is what happened that day. A boy came into the hospital with his family with a bad heart. He needed a heart right away or he would die. The hospital staff checked around but nothing was available. Then they got lucky, for a lack of a better word, because after being unsuccessful in saving Mr. Smith's life, they realized that he was a match for the boy. Since Mr. Smith had no ID, they chose not to wait for any records to find out whether he was a donor or not. The boy didn't have much time. Dr. Cashion knew the risk he was taking when he did this thing, but he wanted to save the little boy's life. So he did what he had to do. John Smith allowed someone to go on living. You can't do anything better than that in society. Thank you. No further questions, Your Honor."

"Do you care to cross examine?" asked the judge, looking at the prosecutor.

"Yes, Your Honor. Thank you, " the prosecutor said as she finished writing her notes.

"Did you say you sold drugs and Dr. Cashion was a valued customer?"

He moved his head up and down in agreement.

"Objection! Please tell the client to speak out loud."

"Counselor, please have your witness say his answers out loud."

"Yes, " Ted said, feeling uncomfortable, for he realized that he may just have convicted himself.

"Do you realize that you must be convicted for telling us this?"

He nodded his head, replied, "Yes, " and looked down.

The prosecutor looked at him with pride. "So keeping your word means that much to you? You know, you have just done two things." Ted looked at the prosecutor, wondering what he had just done. "First, you defined a good friend, and second, you gave us proof that the doctor had a drug problem and needed money to maintain his habit. But before we get back to that, can you tell the court in one sentence or briefly how you started selling drugs?"

"Objection!"

"Your Honor, I'm only trying to bring in a better picture of my witness."

"I will allow it, but please make it very brief."

"I told my mother that if anything happened to Dad, I would take care of her."

"Well, did anything happen to your dad?"

"Yes."

"What happened?"

Chapter 39

Why Ted Became a Drug Dealer

"You are one lousy wife! I asked you one thing, and you do this!" Ted's dad reached back to slap his wife. "You know what? You are not even worth the power in this slap, so I will keep it to myself!"

Ted was a growing teenager, and he had heard things like this since he was young. You see, his father was a hard-working man, but he never felt that he brought home enough money. His father promised his mother that he would be a good father and would always provide everything that was needed. All she had to do was have his children. Well, she was only able to have one, but that was good, because Mr. Humphrey had problems keeping food on the table with just them. Things flared up when he realized that his wife made more money than he did. He wanted her to quit her job as a cashier at the local market, but he knew that that would take food away from Ted. So she kept her job and ended up getting a direct deposit. She lied and told her husband that she had been demoted to make him feel better. That was the only lie Ted ever heard her tell.

Because of her lie, things got better in a sense. For a long time, there was no arguing or fussing. Ted's father felt good because he thought he was the bread-winner. He was impressed by the way his wife budgeted the money. But soon, he figured out that she still made a little more money than he did. First, he thought that she earned more by working late and taking side jobs. Unfortunately or fortunately, she was made head cashier and received higher pay.

Ted's dad was furious and decided to take matters into his own hands. One day, he was sitting on the porch and Ted decided to join him.

"Hi, Dad. What's up?"

"Hey man!"

"Why do you sound so down? Where is Mama?"

"I guess she is working overtime."

"Why do you look so sad?"

"Well, your mama is thinking about leaving me."

"For real?" Ted said with a little smirk.

"Yeah, for real! Are you happy or sad?"

"I am sad, Dad."

"Man, don't lie to me. I know that I haven't been the best dad. As a matter of fact, son, here is a bit of advice coming from your daddy. Remember it always, and make sure you stick by it. A man is only respected for his word. If his word is good, then he will always be respected as a man. So, in your life, be a man who strictly stands by his word."

There was a long pause as Ted took in the knowledge his father had just bestowed on him. His dad stood up.

"Where are you going, asked Ted?"

"I'm going to the store."

"Can I go with you?"

"No, son. You stay back and watch out for when your mother gets home. I will be back," he said, sounding nervous.

Minutes later, Ted's mother came home with three friends from work.

"Hi Mom."

"Hi! Where is your dad?"

"He went to the store. Why are these men here?"

"Stop asking questions and let me see how fast you can pack a suitcase."

"Where are we going?"

"Didn't I just tell you to stop asking so many questions? Go and get your things now. As a matter of fact, here!" She reached into her pocket and pulled out a piece of paper on which she had written something earlier. It has a list of things that Ted should bring. "Can one of you go with him to make sure he packs everything?" she said to one of her friends.

Moments later, Ted's dad walked up the stairs and stood on the porch.

"Who in the hell are all of you?"

"We are friends of your wife," said one of the men.

"Where is she? And who does she think she is, bringing y'all to my house?"

He started wrestling with the two fellows and eventually calmed down. He wanted to speak to his wife.

"Hold on! Can I just say a couple of things?" he asked, upset.

Each of the men held one of Mr. Humphrey's arms and escorted him into the house. He looked at his wife and sighed.

"Woman, where are you going?"

"I am leaving. I will be back to get the rest of my stuff later." The third guy entered the room holding his son.

"Man, let my son go!"

He attempted to go after Ted, but he was held back by the two guys. Ted's dad took a breath and looked at his wife.

"Can we talk alone in the other room?"

"Do you really think I am going to be alone with you when you've been drinking?"

"How are you going to afford a motel or hotel?"

"I saved a lot of money. You see, whether you know it or not, I was making a lot more money than you thought. Now my boss is going to make me manager of the store, and I know that wouldn't be your cup of tea."

"Well, baby, I've been thinking. I don't want you to go, and—"

She cut him off. "Whatever you were about to say, keep it! Don't wait until I get enough nerve to leave and then decide to be all apologetic."

"Well, if you've made up your mind ..."

She moves her head in agreement.

"Then keep your stuff here. I'll do the leaving. I can't have my boy living in the streets. I won't bother you ever. All right?" said Ted's dad.

"Yeah, right!"

"Do you all mind letting me get some of my things?"

The two men looked at each other and then at Ted's mom. She nodded her head in agreement.

Ted's dad walked past her. By this time, Ted was confused and upset. He ran to his dad and gave him a big hug.

"Don't go, Dad."

"Son, your mother appears to have made up her mind. She needs a real man to take care of her."

Ted's mother thought, *You are so right.*

Ted was sad, but he let his father go and watched him walk into the bedroom and close the door.

Mr. Humphrey started rummaging through his things in the room. Mrs. Humphrey thought that this would be a perfect time to escape. She motioned to her son and escorts to move towards the door and looked around to make sure she had everything. Meanwhile, Ted's dad looked in the closet for the gun he had placed there.

Apparently, Ted's mom had hidden it. But Mr. Humphrey didn't give up. He glanced at the chest in which she kept her out-of-season clothes, popped it open, and looked through it. He stumbled over the box that held his gun. But he also noticed some pictures. He put the box to the side and started to sift through the pictures. What he saw, he didn't like.

He wanted to scream, *This is why you are leaving me!*

Mr. Humphrey saw her hugging a man closely who he thought he recognized. There were pictures of his wife and this man at hotels and bars. *Those must have been taken when she said she was working late,* he thought, sighing. He couldn't take it anymore and rushed out of the room to face his wife, but the house was empty.

Ted's dad became even more furious. He rushed back to the room to get his gun, jumped in his car, and drove off. He had no idea where she went. After a while, he passed by the store where his wife worked and noticed a car parked in front. He also noticed a clerk taking out the trash. The manager was probably going to close soon.

"Hey, Trish can you throw the trash away?" the manager asked the closing clerk to do.

When the clerk returned, Mr. Humphrey ran up behind her and whispered, "Be quiet! This is a stickup!"

The clerk did what she was told to do. The manager was counting things on the shelves when he heard someone walk inside.

"Hey! Is that you? Did you lock the door?" There was silence. The man turned away from the shelves and saw a gun pointed at him. "Hey! Hey! Hey! What are you doing?"

"No! That's not the question. The question is what are you doing with my wife?" Mr. Humphrey tossed the pictures at him.

"Hey, man! We are just friends."

"Man! Those pictures show more than just friends. Get your butt over there and don't move," he said, waving the gun in the direction where he wanted him to walk.

As he stumbled over the merchandise in the floor, Mr. Humphrey picks up a bottle of whisky. "Hey, man! What's your name?"

"Curtis," he whispered.

"Louder! I said what's your name?"

"Curtis Byrd," responded the nervous manager.

"What? I think she almost called me that name one day. " He pistol-whipped the man. "You see what you made me do? I bet you are the reason why she is leaving me."

Moments later, they heard a knock at the door. "Is everything all right in there?" a cop called out as he peeped through the glass doors.

"What's that cop doing here?" asked Mr. Humphrey.

"A neighborhood cop always comes around to make sure that the store is closed safely," said Trish the store clerk.

"Get rid of him! " Mr. Humphrey commanded.

"Hey, Mr. Byrd!" the cop called again.

Then he noticed the clerk's shoes coming around the corner of the aisle. By the look on her face, he could tell that something was wrong. He called for backup and cut off his radio. The clerk opened the door for him.

"Is everything all right?" the cop asked as he put his foot inside the door so the clerk couldn't close it.

"We just got a late closing today."

"Where is Mr. Byrd?"

"He's in the back." she winked.

"Okay. Tell him I said hi. I may be back after I check on the other stores, alright?" He winked back at her.

The clerk closed the door, pretended to lock it, and winked again to inform the cop that she hadn't locked the door. Then she returned to where Ted's dad was holding Mr. Byrd.

"Is he gone?" asked Mr. Humphrey.

She nodded her head to say yes.

"Did you lock the door?"

"Yes."

"Come with me. Let me make sure."

They all walked to the front of the store. Then Trish was getting more nervous. When Mr. Humphrey reached out to check the door, it was locked.

"All right. She was telling the truth. I guess you really care about your boss's life — and yours too for that matter."

"Here! Call her."

"Call who?"

"Man, don't act like you don't know who I am speaking of! My wife! And don't act like you don't know the number, because she claimed that her phone belonged to the store. So, here! Call her."

Mr. Byrd called Mr. Humphrey's wife, hoping she would say something to make her husband put down the gun.

"Here! Give me the phone." Mr. Humphrey grabbed the phone and held it to his ear until someone picked it up.

"Hey! We are at the Comfort Inn, " said Ted's mom as soon as she answered the phone.

"Comfort Inn ... huh!"

"Hello? Who is this?"

"Surprise! I got your man held up here at the store. Why don't you come down to get him?"

"What are you doing?"

"I found the pictures, and it is not right the way you are hugged up all over him like that."

"Well, when was the last time you hugged me?"

"This is not about me. It's about you and your cheating habits."

"Honey, I am sorry. Please don't do anything crazy."

"Don't do anything crazy? I told you a long time ago that if anybody was going to come between us, it was going to be over my dead body!"

"No! No! No! " she shouted.

At that moment, the manager noticed the cop standing in the corner with his finger over his mouth to make sure Mr. Byrd stayed quiet.

"Do you want to hear what it sounds like when your new man is shot?" He pointed the gun at Mr. Byrd.

"Police! Put down the weapon." yelled the cop as he jumped out of the corner.

Mr. Humphrey whirled around, and the cop shot him dead on the spot. The room became silent. The only noise was the sound of Mrs. Humphrey screaming through the telephone.

"Mrs. Humphrey, calm down," the manager said in his calmest voice.

"Are you all right?"

"Yes."

"Is my husband all right?"

He handed the phone to the cop.

"Hello."

"Hello. I asked you a question. Is my husband okay?"

"Ma'am, he has been shot."

She bellowed a loud cry.

"Ma'am, I need you to calm down. Is there someone with you who I can speak to?"

She handed the phone to one of the men who helped her leave home. Ted looked at his mother, worried. He knew that his dad would go overboard to stand for what he believed in.

"Hello."

"Hello. Hey, this is the on-duty policeman at the market. Who are you?"

"Mike Yogaphit." One of Mrs. Humphrey's helpers replied.

"Mike Yogaphit?"

"Hey! He oversees all the stock in the store," said Mr. Byrd. "Let me speak to him."

The cop handed the phone back to Mr. Byrd.

"Mike, tell Mrs. Humphrey that her husband has been hurt and he is on his way to the hospital. Tell her to meet us there. Is that her son?"

"Yeah," Mike responded.

"Can someone take care of him? This may be too much for him to handle."

Mr. Byrd said concerned about young Ted.

He hung up the phone, turned around, and looked at the cop who was checking Mr. Humphrey's pulse. The cop looked disappointed.

He reached in the man's pocket for his identification. At the same time, they could hear the ambulance coming. The clerk ran outside to guide them in.

Ted's dad was pronounced dead on arrival at the hospital. When Ted heard the news, the only thing he could remember was the last thing his father told him: Always be a man of your word.

From that moment on, this was the motto by which Ted lived his life.

Chapter 40

Back in Court

Ted was ready to share his life with the court. He wanted to use as few words as possible. "Well, after my father was murdered, my mother became mentally unstable, because she felt that his death was her fault. She quit her job because she didn't want to work at the place where her husband's life had been taken. She had problems keeping other jobs because everywhere she tried, someone tried to date her, especially when they found out she was single. So she was in and out of jobs."

"I remember one day returning from class at the local junior college where I was studying auto mechanics. She was crying because there was a foreclosure on our house. She really didn't want to lose the house. I knew then that I had to do what I needed to do. I ran to the only person I knew who would have the kind of money we needed. My mother swallowed her pride and took the money from me. She constantly said that she would repay whoever I borrowed the money from with interest. I told her not to worry about it. That is how I went to work for a drug dealer. He liked me because I was a man of my word. I started as a drop-off man. But once the customers started to trust me and like me, they began to ask for me personally. I guess they knew I was a quick, reliable deliverer. Anyway, the dealer was put away and someone needed to take his place. He asked me to take care of things if anything ever happened to him. I told him I would, because I had never seen my mother happier. I had paid off my debt a longtime ago."

The prosecutor said, "So you started selling drugs to keep your word? You are a good man." She turned to the jury. "Court, although there are other ways to make ends meet, I think my client was not aware of those resources. Please don't judge him unless you have walked in his shoes." She gave the jury a sincere look. "No further questions, Your Honor."

"Do you care to cross examine?" asked the judge staring at the defendant.

"Thank you, judge," responded the defendant's lawyer. "You know it's really a pity how you are judging the jury's intelligence and trying to get them to feel sorry for this witness. He is a menace—"

"Objection!" the prosecuting attorney cut in.

"Sustained," replied the judge.

"Well, he said it himself, and I quote: 'I use to

sell drugs.' Well, how do we know he's not still at it? How are you getting by now Mr. Ted Humphrey?"

"I make it."

"Off your drug money, I'm sure."

"Objection! The defense is making assumptions," said the prosecutor.

"Sustained."

"Are you working now?"

"I do side jobs here and there."

"Side jobs. Hmmm. " The defense attorney pinched his lips together with wide eyes showing disbelief. "No further questions, Your Honor."

"Care to redirect, plaintiff?" asked the judge.

"No. No, thank you. The plaintiff rests."

"Do we think we can be prepared for closing arguments at noon?" asked the judge, looking at the plaintiff.

The plaintiff shrugged her shoulders and nodded her head. "Yes, Your Honor," she said.

He then turned to the defendant. He agreed as well.

The judge announced the four-hour break and said that everybody should be back that afternoon at one o'clock sharp.

Chapter 41

Relieved and Going to a New Home

"Hello Mrs. Johnson. This is Phil, the social worker at the residential home."

"Hi. Is something wrong?"

"No, no, no. As a matter of fact, everything looks good. You should be taking Fred home soon."

"Oh! In that case, I need to tidy up the house."

"Well, do you think you will mind if he receives visits from his father's friend?"

Mrs. Johnson was silent.

The social worker broke the silence. "Would you like to meet him first?"

"I think that would be wise."

"Well, he planned a trip to take Fred to McDonald's and a movie. Would you like to go? He asked me to ask you. He is very a nice person. I think his work is in sales, but I guess you can ask.

"I think that would be wised."

"Well, he planned a trip to take Fred to McDonald's and a movie. Would you like to go? He asked me to ask you. He is very a nice person. I think his work is in sales, but I guess you can ask him when you see him."

"I guess," Mrs. Johnson said, feeling unsure.

"So, how does Saturday look for you?"

"At what time?"

"I guess for the seven o'clock show."

"Well, I guess so, " she responded, still sounding unsure.

"Okay then. It's settled. Do you think you can meet him here at the center? Then you can all take off from here."

"I guess that's cool."

"Take care, Mrs. Johnson."

"Wait a minute! Can I speak to Fred?"

"Hold on. I will see if he is available."

While Mrs. Johnson held the line, she glanced at the news on TV. The news anchor was just reporting that Dallas won the game. Of course, she started thinking of her man and her son and how they used to fight over the game.

"Hello. Hello." Fred was on the phone and he tried to get her attention.

"Hello. Hey! How are you doing?"

"Fine. Thank you for asking. How are you today?"

"My, you sound all professional."

"Thank you. We just had an etiquette class."

"Oh! I see you were paying attention."

"Yes. I want to make you a good son."

"Just be yourself. You know that guy who comes to see you from time to time?"

"Yes. You are talking about my father's friend, Mr. Ted. What about him?"

"I guess you like him a lot, huh? Tell me, do you know what kind of work he does?"

"Well, I don't know. He says that he is in between jobs. But Mr. Phil says he is in sales."

"Oh, okay. He told me the same thing."

"Mrs. Johnson — or can I call you mother?" Fred waited anxiously for a response.

"Well, let's wait for the papers to clear and for you to be here at my home."

"Okay, but I don't think Ted does anything wrong. My father didn't deal with men like that."

"Well, okay. I will take your word for it. Do you know about going to the movies this Saturday?"

"Yes. You are going, right?" Fred asked, excited.

"Yes, I plan to go."

"Good! That way you can meet him. I think you will like him. " Fred sounded confident.

"I will see you later. Good-bye."

"Good-bye. I am going to check the paper and see what's playing."

"Good for you! Talk to you later."

Chapter 42

The Verdict

When court resumed, the judge called the defense to give its closing argument. Their main points were the fact that Dr. Cashion had never given money in exchange for the alleged attempted murder of the detective and that the detective was crooked for using a drug dealer as a witness. The prosecution's closing argument centered on the issues leading to a conspiracy between Dr. Cashion and Ted Humphrey. Whereas Dr. Cashion was deliberately at the scene to have the detective murdered.

After hearing the closing arguments, the judge dismissed the jury to discuss the case amongst themselves and told them to call him as soon as they reached a decision.

A reporter questioned the prosecutor. "So, where do you think this case is going?"

She looked at him and sighed. "Well, I do think the defense had a strong case. But hopefully, the jury will see things our way."

"Do you think that there will be a mistrial?" "No. If there is, we will try to convict Dr. Cashion for one of his other crimes."

"You know, this would make a good book." "Yeah, maybe we can get an author like Rovel D. Simmons to write it."

"Yeah, right! You wish."

"Ha, ha, ha! " they both laughed.

Silence followed until a loud voice carried through the hallway. "Excuse me, everyone! The jury has come to a decision."

"Wow! That was fast," said the prosecutor.

"It sure was! What does that normally mean?" asked the reporter.

"It normally means not guilty, but let's see," replied the prosecutor.

Everyone walked back into the courtroom and took their seats, discussing what they thought the verdict would be.

"I'll bet you twenty dollars he is not guilty," a member of the audience said to his friend beside him.

"It's a bet! Everything pointed to him, including things that had nothing to do with the case. He was a bad doctor and he should burn," his friend responded with confidence.

"We will see."

"All rise!" shouted the bailiff when he saw the judge's door open.

"Thank you. You may all be seated," said the judge. "Bailiff, please let the jury in."

"Yes sir, " responded the bailiff.

He turned to open the jurors' door. The twelve jurors entered the courtroom, one behind the other, looking straight and serious. They all took their seats.

"Jury, do you have the verdict?" asked the judge.

"Yes, Your Honor," responded the head juror.

The judge looked at the bailiff. He took the verdict from the head juror and placed it on the judge's desk.

"Thank you. Next time, put it in my hand," instructed the judge.

"Sorry, Your Honor. And you are welcome."

The judge read the paper quickly and handed it back to the bailiff. He returned it to the head juror. When the judge saw that the bailiff was back in his usual spot, he asked the defendant to stand while the verdict was read.

"Please read the verdict," said the judge.

"We, the jurors, find the defendant, Dr. Bill Cashion, on count one of using drugs which violates the Hippocratic Oath and puts people lives in danger. Not guilty."

The doctor sat with no expression. His lawyer whispered something in his ear.

"On count number two, of conspiracy to kill a policeman, we, the jury, find the defendant guilty as charged."

A few members of the audience expressed

remarks. One person gleamed and held his hand out, whispering, "Pay me! Pay me! " The judge quickly quieted everyone by pounding the table with his mallet.

"The court rests," said the judge. "Sentencing will take place tomorrow morning at ten o'clock."

The next day, the court sentenced the doctor to ten years in prison. Ted was upset that the sentence was so mild.

Man! If I'd been on trial, I would have got life! He thought as he listened to the judge's last remarks. When the bailiff excused the crowd, he wasted no time before calling Mrs. Johnson to give her the news.

Chapter 43

Can I Call You Back?

After Ted and Mrs. Johnson went to the movies, of course they went to McDonald's. It was there that they had gotten to know each other. It was ironic that they knew some of the same people. They were really surprised when they found out that they both despised Dr. Cashion and felt that he needs to pay for his crimes. Anyway, Mrs. Johnson felt that it will be wise to keep Ted around for Fred. So she swallowed her pride and didn't even care to share about her involvement with the killing of his friend. On the other hand, Ted didn't bother to share his involvement with the disappearing of her husband. They both felt that it will be better for their friendship and for Fred if they kept certain things to their selves.

Meanwhile, Ted is walking out the court room with his cell phone to his ear. "He only got ten years!" Ted said into the phone as soon as Mrs. Johnson answered it.

"Well, he got something! I am so glad this chapter in your life and perhaps my life is over," she said. "Too bad my husband is not here for this."

"Yeah" Ted replied softly.

There was silence on the phone for five seconds. "Can I call you back?" Ted asked, breaking the silence.

"Is everything all right? I mean you don't sound too happy?"

"Yeah, everything is cool. I will call you later; I have to make another phone call."

"All right. Good bye."

Ted pushes the speed dial and tries to contact the person he asked to take care of Mr. Johnson.

"Who dis, " responded Brent, the hit man.

"This Ted."

"Crazy Ted, man what's up with you? No wonder I didn't recognize your number! I erased your phone number from my phone that same day you were talking crazy."

"I hope you are not asking for another hit to be done."

"No?"

"Yo man, then why the call? I know you just don't want to talk. You know me and you don't have anything to talk about. You are too iffy for me. I mean, first you want someone knocked off, and then you don't."

"Man, I need your help." Ted said softly.

A brief moment of silence.

"You know what? If it wasn't for you, I wouldn't be in this great situation anyway —you hooking me up with that rich man."

"Yeah, that's what I need to talk to you about. How come they never found his body? I mean, have you done this kind of work before, because you are good. I would assume by now a dog or something would have come across it."

"Well, let me just say I got skills," the hitman responded with confidence.

"Man, come on! Tell me the truth. I need to know, because I am interested in hooking up with his wife, and I don't want anything to happen."

"Well, check this out, now! I heard you got out of the game."

"Yeah, I did."

"Good for you, because I did flee the area after I did what I am about to tell you."

"What?"

"You are trying to stay out of trouble, because if this leaks out, I will tell on you and everybody else."

"Man, whatever! What's up?"

"Well, remember when I told you about how Johnson offered us more money not to shoot him, but we did anyway?"

"Yeah, I remember," Ted responded,

remembering the day at the adoption home with Fred and how excited he was when he thought he had a new father.

"Well, then he offered us more money to act like we'd shot him and that he was dead. He said the doctor would tell on him if he got caught, and he had an idea that the detective was getting close to solving the case. You guys never found his body because he rolled out somewhere overseas. He said that he was going to wait until all this stuff cooled off before he returned for his family."

"Well, if he has been watching the news, he will realize that it's all cooled off because the doctor was convicted of that crime." replied Ted.

"Well, I am sure by this time, he probably has his own thing going on. I mean I am not gay or nothing, but he was a rich, cool-looking guy. So, I am sure he got his own business and a flock of women by now."

"You didn't kill him right?"

"Right."

"That's all I needed to know," said Ted.

He hung up the phone and quickly dialed Mrs. Johnson back.

She never picked up the phone, so he rushed over to her house.

Chapter 44

Falling

Ted pulled up in front of Mrs. Johnson's home. At the same time, Mrs. Johnson was pulling up the driveway without even noticing that Ted had arrived. When she got out the car, Fred saw Ted getting out of the driver's seat of his car, and Fred attacked him, planting a big hug on him.

"Wow! I guess you are happy to see me, " Ted said, picking Fred up and hugging him back.

"Hi Ted, " Mrs. Humphrey said, picking up a bag of groceries. "Fred take the rest of these bags inside so I can talk to Ted."

Fred ran into the house with several loads of groceries.

"What's going on? Why the surprise visit?"

"Give me this." he takes the groceries out of her hand and handed it to Fred who just returned from dropping off a load of groceries.

"You know, I was just thinking-it's been a year since Reggie's disappearance. If he was coming back, he would have been back by now. I wish they would have found his body so I can get closure. I am ready to move on with my life. Yeah, I did dislike some of his ways but he was my husband. God says that it's not right to hate. But in this case of someone trying to hurt my husband I might have to beg to differ. But anyway, I'm just rambling. Didn't you have something you wanted to say?"

"Ah, no! " Ted said as he thought about what he was getting ready to share.

"Well, what did you come over here for?"

Ted said the first thing that came to his mind to get off the subject.

"I came to see you."

"Ah that's so sweet. You know what, if I wasn't married or if Reggie wasn't ... well you know; you'd be a good catch." Mrs. Johnson said, contemplating the thought of being with him.

Ted blushes.

"Speaking of which," Mrs. Johnson continued with the other thought popping into her head. "I wonder how long I have to wait before I can start seeing other people or get married again for that matter. We should go to the court one day to find out the law for marriages when someone is missing."

Ted nods his head still smiling from the compliment. Fred comes running back and starts play hitting Ted.

"Are you coming to watch movies with us?" he asked, while Ted threw him on the ground and put him in a wrestling move.

Ted looked at Mrs. Johnson while on the ground.

"I guess that will be fine." she responded with a smile.

"Cool! We got two movies." said an excited Fred.

"Fred, we've got to eat dinner first. Afterwards, we will watch the movie. Now Ted let him up. We don't want him to get dirty." Mrs. Johnson said helping Fred up and dusting him off.

After their meal, Fred and Ted went to the front room to watch movies while Mrs. Johnson went to her room to talk to herself and God.

God, please let my husband be all right. I know you are watching over him. I will wait for a sign about whether I should really move on with my life. She paused and thoughts of Ted crossed her mind. *Wow! Where did that come from?*

She brushed the thought back out of her mind. "Amen."

She heard laughter coming from the front room.

She went to see what was so funny. When she walked down the hallway and saw Ted and Fred laughing and having so much fun watching the movie, her imagination wondered how it would be.

"Stop it! Stop it! " she chided herself aloud. "I

am still married. But I am falling for this guy. " Her eyes were teary.

Later that year, there is still no sign of Mr. Johnson. Mrs. Johnson and Ted were interested in dating each other, but before things got too serious, they decided to go to the courthouse to see if she could get a divorce without her husband's consent. When the clerks found her records, they saw that her papers had never been completed. They realized that they weren't signed by an ordained minister. Ted smiled and looked at Mrs. Johnson, hoping that she would smile with him.

"Ted, I don't want to smile. Think! All this time, I've been thinking I was married and I find out I've never been. You know, I wondered why his friend did our sermon, but I kept my mouth shut, thinking that he had things taken care of. I am so tired of him thinking his money will solve everything. Dude! Can you believe that I am not even married?"

She looks at Ted, who showed a wide smile.

"Well, we can take care of that right now, " he said.

And he got down on one knee.

Chapter 45

This Is for Our Protection

Another year had gone by, and there was still no word from Mr. Johnson. Ted and Mrs. Johnson decided to move away. Ted felt that there was too much dirt on him in this city and Mrs. Johnson felt that there were too many memories. They packed boxes getting ready for the movers who are supposed to be there in a minute. Ted turns the television on after looking at his watch realizing that it's almost time for the news. He wanted to get the forecast to see if the roads will be clear.

Fred was in the back, packing things from the junk closet. He opened an old looking shoebox. Inside was a gun. Fred picks up the gun and looked through the sight, aiming it at a lamp. He starts imagining that the lamp is the person who killed his father.

If I had that chance! He thought.

Ted walked in, said Fred playing with the gun,

and started to yell. But he was afraid that his raised voice might scare him and set the gun off. Approaching him from the back, Ted took carefully gauged steps towards Fred. He put his hand on the gun barrel gently laying a hand on Fred's shoulders.

"Here! Give me this. This is for our protection in case anyone tries to come in on us."

Ted placed the gun back in the box.

"Now agree with me—no, promise me that you won't touch this unless it's to protect us."

Ted and Fred extended their hands and they shook on it.

"Ahhhing! " screamed Mrs. Johnson from the kitchen.

She had just cut her hand on a piece of glass. Ted dropped the box with the gun in it on the nightstand. He and Fred ran to see what was wrong.

"Are you okay?" they said simultaneously.

"No, I just cut my hand."

Ted grabbed her wrist and rushed it to the sink.

"Can you get me a towel?" he asked Fred while the water ran on the cut.

Fred handed him a towel that he saw in one of the boxes.

"Thank you. Here! Let's dry your hand, so that we can see how deep the cut is."

"I don't think it's so deep that I am going to need stitches," said Mrs. Johnson.

"All right, I guess you're right," Ted responded after looking closely at the cut.

"Fred, go into the room and look for the bandages by the nightstand, " asked Ted.

"All right."

Ted walked back to the kitchen and started putting the rest of Mrs. Johnson's dishes in the box. As he placed them inside, he heard the TV. The news was about to come on.

"Did you hear all the ambulance sirens in the streets today?" asked Mrs. Johnson.

"Do you think they are coming for you?" Ted asked her sarcastically.

Mrs. Johnson narrowed her eyes and smirks.

"Ted I'll—"

"Shhh! " Ted said as he put one finger over his lip to listen to the television.

"Did you hear that?"

"Hear what?" she asked.

"They just said on the news that a doctor just got out of prison after spending two years there."

"Do you think it's Dr. Cashion?" asked Mrs. Johnson, looking worried.

"I hope not."

"I wonder how long he has been out, " she said. "I guess we will find out in a few minutes."

"Hey! What's taking Fred so long with those bandages?"

"Ah, crap! I left that box with the gun in it on the table! I'd better check on him."

"No! I will check on him. You finish watching the news for that story."

The news came back on and the doctor's story was the first item.

"This is just in. After a retrial ..."

"Hey! It's back on, " Ted yelled.

"Okay! I am looking for Fred. Hey, where did you say that box was? " Mrs. Johnson replied.

"A doctor was released today after spending two years in prison," the news reporter continued. "We will give you more details coming up at 11:00. Again, Dr. Cashion was released from prison today after a retrial. The court stated that it was unconstitutional to entrap the doctor."

Ted stood there with wide eyes.

He heard a knock at the door. Ted answered it, still stunned and thinking it's the movers. When he opened the door, he was even more surprised to see who was there. Mrs. Johnson walked in from the back room.

"Honey, I can't find ..."

She paused and her eyes also widened when she saw who was standing at the door. At that moment, the man swings at Ted and he ducks and grabs the man slamming him on the floor. Fred heard the commotion and ran in from the back room thinking about the agreement—or was it a promise?

"This is for our protection!"

THE END

www.ingramcontent.com/pod-product-compliance
Lightning Source LLC
Chambersburg PA
CBHW070121260626
47160CB00004B/1572